MURDER HAPPENS

Jim Courter

MURDER HAPPENS

HISTRIA
FICTION

Histria Fiction

Las Vegas ◊ Chicago ◊ Palm Beach

Published in the United States of America by
Histria Books
7181 N. Hualapai Way, Ste. 130-86
Las Vegas, NV 89166 USA
HistriaBooks.com

Histria Fiction is an imprint of Histria Books. Titles published under the imprints of Histria Books are distributed worldwide.

This is a work of fiction. Names, characters, places, and incidents are either the product of the author's imagination or are used fictitiously. Any resemblance to actual persons, living or dead, is entirely coincidental.

Library of Congress Control Number: 2024931096

ISBN 978-1-59211-479-5 (softbound)
ISBN 978-1-59211-492-4 (eBook)

All is seared with trade.

— Gerard Manley Hopkins

CHAPTER 1
ALPHA

The walkers were strung out around the cruciform perimeter of the mall, some in pairs and chattering away, the solitary ones leaning into it with the grim determination of one trying to stay a step ahead of the Reaper. In spite of having witnessed that parade for over fifteen years, I was struck that morning for the first time by the symbolism of their going counterclockwise.

Leo and I were at a table on the terrace between Lincoln Court and the inside entry to Lincoln Inn. A retiree like most of the walkers, Leo kept his distance from them, having little patience with their gossip, complaining, and, sometimes, maudlin foolishness.

"According to this, Cleary," Leo said from behind his *Chicago Tribune*, "Joe Whitehead showed up in Peoria yesterday wearing a bulletproof vest."

I lowered my *News-Gazette*. "Tell me more," I said.

"Says he's been getting death threats but vows to continue his campaign for the governorship — I'm quoting here — 'undeterred and unbullied.'"

Whitehead had recently announced that he was moving his campaign headquarters from his home base in the suburbs to Downstate, and his stop in Peoria was the first in his search for a location. His next stop was Lincoln Court, any moment now if he was on schedule. Why he would consider an undersized and failing shopping mall was beyond me, but already some merchants were pressuring Art Ziemann, Lincoln Court's manager, to offer him a sweet deal in the hope that his presence might somehow tip the balance in favor of survival. If he did choose Lincoln Court, and if it was true that he had received death threats, I'd be curious to know what might be expected of me. I had busted my share of shoplifters, managed to keep the homeless from making the mall their home, even rousted the occasional bathroom dope smoker, but I was fairly certain that protecting a politician from an assassin's bullet wasn't in my job description.

I went back to reading the *News-Gazette*. The shops would open in ten minutes. Art had moved back Sunday's opening time to get the jump on Prairieview Shopping Center in Champaign, which opened at noon, and perhaps to squeeze a few coins from the Brethren, whose services in the Community Room on the lower level ended at eleven o'clock. Art had been desperate for any competitive advantage since the announcement by Craddock's, Lincoln Court's anchor and only department store, that it would close for good at the end of the year or when inventory was liquidated, whichever came first.

Across the way, Eddie Braun lifted the security grate halfway up in front of his jewelry store, ducked under it, and emerged onto the concourse with a mug of coffee. A flat gold chain visible through the open collar of his black silk shirt, diamonds on his left pinkie and left ear, hair slicked back and shiny, Eddie could have been a wiseguy in a Scorcese film. He came across and stood on the other side of the railing, effectively joining Leo and me at our table.

"Another damn day," Eddie said. He gestured with his coffee mug to indicate the walkers. "Look at this sorry bunch — fossils on fixed incomes, and I'm pushing high-end merchandise."

Bob, in coveralls, trundled up from around the corner with his cleaning cart and stopped near Eddie. Eddie slid a finger along the underside of the gold chain and scanned like radar over Bob's head.

"Food's as good as gone," Eddie said. "As of January one we'll be without an anchor. I guarantee you, if nobody fills that space it'll be plywood over the windows and weeds in the parking lot."

Bob shook his head and made a ticking noise with a corner of his mouth. "It's like I always say," he said, but, as usual with Bob, it was unclear what he always said or what was *like* what he always said.

"I took in seventy-five dollars yesterday," Eddie said, "less than that the day before. This keeps up, I'm headed for Prairieview, high rent or no. At least I can make a living there."

"The wife's out to Prairieview just about every day," Bob said. "She says the place is full up."

"Businesses come and go," Eddie said. "My lease expires in five months, and I'm on Prairieview's waiting list. Art knows it, too. He cuts me some slack on a new lease or I'm out of here. Maybe I'm out of here anyway."

"You should move to downtown Champaign," Leo said. "There's no jewelry there since Raskins pulled out."

"If I didn't know better," Eddie said, "I'd think you were trying to get rid of me." Eddie reached across the railing and took hold of Leo's left pinkie. "Nice rock. You have good taste for an old fart."

Leo pulled his hand away and shielded himself from Eddie with his newspaper.

Alice, in her own world, a shopping bag weighing down her right side, appeared from somewhere and sat wearily on a bench in the middle of the concourse and commenced mumbling to herself.

Jess and Margaret passed, a husband-and-wife pair of retired English teachers who walked in the mornings. Eddie smiled at them with a kind of deferential puzzlement, as at members of that mysterious class that value the artistic arrangement of words more highly than gems and precious metals.

"I got a mother in a nursing home," Eddie said. "I got support payments and lady friends with expensive tastes. I can't make a living here anymore."

Some of the Brethren came up the stairs into the sunlight pouring through the fenestrated vault over the south concourse. They squinted, shaded their eyes, and looked around as if just released from prolonged underground confinement. Among them was Mrs. Orville Sharpe, the reverend's wife. She was a massive, formidable woman, and her six children seemed to stay in tow behind her by gravitational pull. The reverend trailed them in his powder-blue, western-cut polyester suit and bola tie. He looked weary and vaguely perturbed; his combover needed combing over. Hard to credit that he was the same man I had heard declaiming with such vehemence only a half hour before as I passed the Community Room, something from Zephaniah about owls hooting through the windows and rubble in the doorways.

"*And the people said...*"

"*Amen!*"

I made a mental note to try to find out if the women among the Brethren were called the Sistern.

Eddie sipped coffee and shook his head. "I got news for you, without an anchor, you don't have a shopping mall." He pointed to where Adolpho was opening his pushcart full of brightly colored baubles, garments, and accessories from Central and South America. "What you got is a flea market!"

"They say if Whitehead gets elected," Bob said, "Roger Worthington'll get the backing he needs to turn this place around like he's been planning."

"*They say!*" Eddie said. "I say we'll be lucky to make it to Christmas and Worthington will go to his grave with those big plans of his still on the drawing board. Besides, Whitehead's a dozen points behind in the polls."

"Ten," Leo said from behind his Trib. "Which may be the least of his problems if somebody out there's got a bullet with his name on it. Speak of the devil."

Joe Whitehead, the Republican candidate for governor, came through the north doors escorted by his retinue, Beth Childress, and some members of the press. They walked down the concourse, stopped for a moment while Beth gestured and spoke, then moved to the center of the mall.

I slugged down the remainder of my coffee, stood, and folded the newspaper under my arm. "Time to go to work," I said.

"You call that work?" Eddie said.

Eddie went back to his store and lifted the security grate all the way up. Bob moved on with his cart. Leo stayed put. I left the terrace and moved to the perimeter of Whitehead's entourage. As I did, Roger Worthington marched through the south entrance, a briefcase in one hand and a tube of blueprints in the other. He shot a look toward the knot of people at the center then took the stairs two at a time up to his office suite overlooking the south concourse.

A young guy in a navy-blue blazer came and stood next to me and looked me up and down, as if trying to assess whether I posed a threat to Whitehead's safety. On that day, as always, I would have had trouble passing for a security guard. When I first hired in, Jerry Burnside, owner of the security firm with which the mall had a contract, gave me an ID badge and said he'd like me to work in slacks and a decent shirt but that I needn't wear a tie or uniform. Since then I've worn the semi-tattered Harris tweed sport coat and one-hundred percent cotton pants and shirt, somewhat rumpled since I didn't own an iron and never sprang for dry cleaning, that I wear virtually everywhere. I got out my ID — DEVIN CLEARY / SECURITY —

and pinned it to a lapel of my sport coat. The guy in the blazer looked at it and wrinkled his nose. He moved off but kept an eye on me.

Reporters fired more or less simultaneous questions at Whitehead. Did he take seriously the threats on his life? Would he speculate on their source? How did he plan to close the double-digit gap in the polls? Was there any truth to the rumor of a deal between him and Roger Worthington — a hefty campaign contribution in return for his support, if he were elected, for Worthington's plans to redevelop and expand Lincoln Court? Why was he moving his campaign headquarters from the suburbs to Downstate?

As Whitehead started to speak, a press guy in the rear yelled one more question.

"Are you wearing a bulletproof vest?"

CHAPTER 2
THE CANDIDATE

In that off-year election of 1986, Joe Whitehead faced challenges that he hadn't faced two years earlier when he won a second term as state senator: He didn't have Ronald Reagan's coattails to ride, and he needed to carry not only his safe, Republican district in the western suburbs, but all of Illinois. That second one probably explained his decision to relocate his campaign headquarters to Downstate. He must have calculated that the Republican suburbs and Democratic Chicago would cancel each other out and that the Downstate vote would determine the outcome.

His Democratic opponent was Illinois Secretary of State Gerald Price. He had a squeaky-clean reputation and occupied the office, with its high visibility and name recognition, that in Illinois had become a stepping stone to the governor's mansion. Most of the smart money was on Price. Perhaps the only drag on his prospects was Tony Quinn, his running mate, a gruff, crude, partisan remnant of the Chicago Democratic machine.

Price's lead in the polls hovered around ten points through the summer. It rose to as high as fifteen when Whitehead's philandering emerged as an issue; fell below ten when the Republicans brushed the cobwebs off corruption charges against Quinn from a decade previous; rose again and leveled off when, at a Cicero American Legion dinner, Whitehead referred to Chicago's West Side as "Gorillaville." It was on the heels of that performance that he showed up in Urbana.

Apparently satisfied that all the questions had been asked, Whitehead spoke.

"I'll save for last the question referring to threats on my life," he said. "As for those poll numbers, I've never been a great believer in polls, but I suppose they tell us something, and what they tell me is that this election will be decided right here, in Downstate Illinois. But of course that's not the main reason I'm here."

For too long, he said, the "honest, hard-working people of Downstate" have been overlooked and taken for granted, this in spite of contributing mightily to a state economy that is larger than that of most countries. He was here "by golly" to see that we got the credit we deserved.

"Now, as for those threats against my person..." He dropped the corners of his mouth, firmed up his chin as best he could, punched the air with a finger. "Joe Whitehead is not about to let cheap thugs interfere with the democratic process. Joe Whitehead doesn't back off from anybody, individual or mob."

His use of that last word suggested that he might be trying to plant the idea that the threats had come from organized crime, which had been making murderous headlines in recent months and against which he had been railing since announcing his candidacy.

If that was Whitehead's intention, I wasn't buying it. The mob wasn't likely to target a guy ten points behind in the polls. It was then and there, in fact, that I began hatching my own theory about the source of those threats.

"As for the question about the bulletproof vest," he went on, "the answer is no, I'm not wearing one. The one I wore in Peoria was on loan from the police there. I'm confident that I don't need one here among the law-abiding folks of Urbana."

His security people seemed less certain of that. The guy who had checked me out, having decided I was harmless, moved watchfully around the fringe of the group. Another, a young jock in sunglasses, conned and rocked on the balls of his feet; he might have been auditioning for a part in an action-adventure film.

Whitehead appeared ready to move on. He still hadn't addressed the question about the rumored deal between him and Roger Worthington. The reporter who had asked it asked again, with studied patience and in measured tones.

"Have you and Roger Worthington made a deal — your backing, if you're elected, for his plans to redevelop and expand Lincoln Court, in return for a hefty contribution to your campaign?"

Before Whitehead could answer, another reporter added one of his own.

"Speaking of that, Senator, is there anything to the talk that says you'll pick your campaign headquarters based on which town's special interests come up with the biggest campaign contribution?"

Whitehead looked stern, as if at impertinent youth. "First, no such deal between me and Mr. Worthington has been made or is in the works. Nor am I aware that he has revealed any plans for this place or indicated when he might do so. I've heard of Lincoln Court's troubles, and it's my sincere hope that they can be overcome, if only for the welfare of the good people whose jobs are at stake. If I can make some small contribution by running my campaign from here, so be it, but I have to weigh other considerations."

He paused and looked straight at the reporter who had piggybacked his question onto the one about Worthington. He arched an eyebrow and swelled his chest.

"Anybody who knows Joe Whitehead," he said, "knows that Joe Whitehead can't be bought. Will politics play a part in my choice? Sure it will. But my main concern is to see that the hard-working people of Downstate Illinois get a fair shake."

All along, Beth Childress had been nodding in earnest, making notes on a pad of paper, conferring in whispers with Whitehead's people. Forgive her, but she now had to remind us that the senator was a busy man. She took him by the elbow, a gesture I knew all too well, and steered him off and away.

I later learned that Whitehead spent that night at Lincoln Inn. The next day he made some stops around town, including one at Prairieview Shopping Center, which although "full up," was also on his list of potential sites, and then was off for Decatur.

After the buzz stirred up by his visit subsided, business at Lincoln Court returned to normal, which is to say not so much back to traffic in money and merchandise as to rumors and speculation on its demise, with one difference: For some, the sliver of hope left in Whitehead's wake changed the question about the ultimate failure and closure of the mall from *when* to *whether*.

CHAPTER 3
A SINKING SHIP

Lincoln Court had begun listing around 1975, when Prairieview Shopping Center opened in the northwest corner of Champaign. Perhaps the only thing that kept it afloat was its proximity to downtown Urbana and the University of Illinois. Students came and shopped, but the group with the most serious buying power were the yuppie TINKS (two incomes, no kids) from the U of I — faculty and staff, researchers, and administrators. Our surveys indicated that they liked the boutique feel of many of Lincoln Court's shops and its smaller size compared to Prairieview, which they disdained for being too large and too commercially crass.

They came mainly in mixed-gender pairs, fit and purposeful in wire-rimmed glasses and dressed in crisp, casual cottons from Eddie Bauer or L. L. Bean. The male usually managed to look both sensitive and intellectually formidable, the female like the first chair in the cello section of the symphony. At Crackers 'n' Crates they agonized over which chocolates to give to Mother the Belgian or the French? Did one have unclean hands in the Third World? And they simply couldn't decide between the Birkenstocks and the Rockports.

The seniors constituted most of the remainder of the traffic. They walked in the mornings before the shops opened, some staying into the day, gabbing and gossiping on the benches. But they did more talking and walking than shopping.

Adding color to the mix were Urbana's marginalized citizens, the homeless and indigent old, who drifted in to seek refuge from the elements, to use the bathrooms, sometimes to panhandle until I or one of my colleagues rousted them. I always found it fascinating that the downtrodden passed in and out of the same doorways as people with international reputations in the arts and sciences. Beth's take on the same phenomenon was to lament that zoning laws didn't prevent the unwashed and uneducated from mingling with more enlightened segments of society.

And so it was that Lincoln Court hung on for more than ten years.

Then in early August of 1986, Craddock's, which accounted for about half the mall's retail square footage, dropped the atomic bomb, announcing that liquidation sales would begin in November and that the store would close at the end of the year at the latest, and maybe sooner.

After that announcement, rats began deserting the ship. Within a month, four more tenants either left or announced their intention to leave. Art Ziemann began positioning pushcarts and kiosks in front of vacant storefronts, the better to mask the malls' plight; it wasn't long before they outnumbered viable storefronts. When Darlene's, a women's apparel store and the biggest draw besides Craddock's, pulled up stakes, one could almost hear the creak of the coffin lid coming down.

All the while, rumors ricocheted like bullets. One had Lincoln Court folding before Craddock's could close; another had a big-name department store chain lined up to take its place.

And then there were the long-awaited and mysterious plans of Roger Worthington to buy out and redevelop and expand Lincoln Court, along with Lincoln Inn, elegant going to shabby. If he had been waiting for its prospects and its price to hit bottom, then surely he must be ready to make his move. (Never mind the opinion held by some that it had no price and never would have, no matter how bad things got, that the Parishes, Lincoln Court's owners, would never give it up or allow it to be altered along the lines Worthington was rumored to have in mind.)

In spite of my personal stake in how things turned out — with no marketable skills to speak of, I faced the possibility of losing the job that had kept me solvent for over fifteen years — I managed to observe the entire affair with a certain amount of amused detachment: Few spectacles elicit less sympathy from me than the desperation of merchants.

It was in the wake of the news of Craddock's imminent closure that Joe Whitehead, a U of I law school graduate, put Lincoln Court on his list of possible sites for his campaign headquarters. Some insiders thought his setting up at the mall might tip the scales in favor of survival by reversing the psychology of doom that had set in; others pointed out that his would be a short-term presence and add nothing to the retail mix. With death threats hanging over his head, some even wondered if he might scare off what few customers we had left. As for the rumors of Worthington's grandiose plans and their linkage to some kind of deal with Whitehead, Worthington had hinted at those plans for so long that he had lost credibility in the eyes of a lot of people. Besides, Whitehead could weigh in on Worthington's behalf only if he were elected governor, and the chances of that looked poor.

Soon after Whitehead's visit, Art told me that he had learned that his people were concerned about security here. He had learned too that the Urbana police put the word out that they shouldn't be counted on to lend a hand with security if Whitehead located at Lincoln Court. Granted, he was a public figure involved in an important public process, but Lincoln Court was private property. And yet, word leaked from Whitehead's camp that he had narrowed his choices, and that Lincoln Court was still in the running.

In the next few weeks, Whitehead returned to town a couple of times to campaign. On one occasion he showed up again at Lincoln Court. It was during that visit that whatever hope remained of his locating here seemed to be dashed. As Beth Childress escorted Whitehead around, an urgent voice at high volume rang through the mall:

"I'll kill 'im. I'll kill the son-of-a-bitch. I get my hands on 'im, I'll kill 'im."

When the flap subsided, we learned that it was mad, homeless Charles, who had frequented the premises between times in jail or in hospital psychiatric wards. He had been put on release again, and upon breathing free air had almost immediately reverted to his schizoid-paranoid self. Useless to argue that Charles was harmless, the newspapers reported that Whitehead's advisors were urging him to drop Lincoln Court from his list.

In mid-August, the Illinois legislature was called back into session to deal with emergency budgetary matters. Whitehead reported to Springfield. As he entered the Senate chamber one morning he told reporters that he would reveal the location of his new campaign headquarters within a few hours.

By the time I got back to my apartment that night after work, I had heard nothing on the subject. I spent the evening reading and scribbling and out of touch with the news. My shift the next day started mid-morning. When I went in, I had still heard nothing about Whitehead's decision. I went to the Lincoln Inn desk, took one each of a *Trib* and a *News-Gazette* from the stacks there and joined Leo on the terrace. He was looking sly. I guessed that he had heard the news but wasn't going to spoil it for me.

The coverage of Whitehead's press conference wasn't on page one of the *Trib*. Schooling myself in patience, I read the front page first and worked my way in until I found it on page four: Joe Whitehead had chosen Lincoln Court for his campaign headquarters. I read it again to make sure I had it right.

He attributed his decision to the affection with which he had come to regard Champaign-Urbana and the U of I since his days as a law student. He admitted that other factors carried some weight but denied, apparently in the face of a direct question, that he had struck a deal with Roger Worthington, insisting that the decision came down to "reasons of the heart." He expected to begin moving in within a week.

I lowered the *Trib* and looked across at Leo.

"Reasons of the heart?" I said.

"Right," Leo said. "And if you believe that, I've got a bridge to sell you."

"It doesn't say here what space he's moving into."

"Darlene's," Leo said. "It's the right size and the right price, this being a renter's market."

Art Ziemann appeared next to me across the railing, looking fretful and burdened. Art always looked fretful and burdened, so I didn't think much of it. He leaned toward me and said almost in a whisper, "I need to see you in my office. Come around eleven o'clock."

CHAPTER 4
A DEATH THREAT

The mall office was a pair of small tandem rooms in the basement, connected by an inner door. Preferring to be left alone and to hear no bad news, Art spent most of his time holed up out of sight in back, while Mindy, his secretary, sat guard out front. Mindy seemed to have figured out that she could distract attention from her incompetence by acting obnoxious, and I suspected that Art had hired her for her repellent effect on people. She made frequent trips to what was left of the shops, to the mall employees' lounge in the basement to watch soap operas on the TV there, or to the bathroom, so I knew there was a good chance I could get to Art without having to pass her. Sure enough, a little after eleven, I went down and found her gone. The door to Art's office was open. I went back and stood in his doorway. Art waved me in. I accepted his invitation to sit.

Art almost never had much to say about my job performance. When I displeased him, which wasn't often, he was distant and frigid; most other times he was distant and opaque. So when he began by commending me on my work, I smelled a rat. With that out of the way, he gave me a weird smile and worked his lips as if he had paste in his mouth.

"Personally," he said, "I wish Whitehead had picked someplace else." He stopped and waited for a response. When I offered none, he went on. "There's no way his setting up shop here will turn this place around. We don't have the staff for it, security-wise."

I sensed that there was more on his mind but that I'd have to pry it out of him if I wanted to learn what it was.

I decided to share my theory about the source of those death threats.

"I could be off in left field on this," I said, "but I've got a hunch somebody in Whitehead's camp, maybe even Whitehead himself, invented those death threats so he could strike a brave pose in the face of them."

At that, Art pursed his lips and arched an eyebrow. He rolled back in his chair, opened the center drawer of his desk, pulled out a sheet of paper folded twice, and handed it across to me. I unfolded it. Near the top in squiggly, hand-scrawled capital letters were these words:

WHITEHEAD WILL DIE HERE

I looked at Art.

"Somebody dropped it through the mail slot in the outer door," he said. "It was there this morning when I came in around nine-thirty. It could have appeared before closing last night. I left around eight."

"Have you told the police?"

"No."

"Do you intend to?"

"No. I'm convinced it's a hoax, probably a copycat who's heard about the threats against Whitehead." The nervousness in his voice suggested less certainty than his words did.

I refolded the sheet and held it out for Art to take. He raised his hands in a defensive gesture, as if it carried plague germs.

"Keep it," Art said. "If something happens, see that the police get it. Mail it anonymously if you want to. Maybe it'll have fingerprints."

Of course it would — Art's and mine.

I slipped the sheet into an inside breast pocket of my sport coat. Art gave me an uncertain look that might have been a smile.

I left, not sure why he had called me in. But as I walked off, mindful of that sheet in the pocket of my sport coat, it occurred to me that he had succeeded in passing a hot item, along with whatever risk and responsibility that attached to it, from him to me. I felt like I'd been had.

CHAPTER 5
MOVE IN DAY

A few days later, trucks backed up to the north concourse doors and disgorged office furniture and supplies, along with computers, copiers, and telephones. Within a short time Darlene's was transformed into what soon became known at the mall as the Whiteheadquarters. Banners and posters went up inside, some bearing the candidate's picture and his campaign slogan:

JOE WHITEHEAD – FOR ALL OF ILLINOIS

The place was staffed mostly by college students spouting political and philosophical positions that require more years than they had lived to properly form. They worked the phones and keyboards, shook hands, distributed literature, and talked the talk to anyone with stomach enough to go in. The mall had a policy against solicitation, and Art, to his credit, decreed that it applied also to politicking, so they were confined to behind the lease line.

After everything was in place, Joe Whitehead showed up on a Friday morning for a sort of grand opening. Short and stocky, with a full head of stiff blond hair going to white and a beefheart complexion, Whitehead had the look of a sybarite and the thrust and strut not so much of a man secure in himself socially, professionally, and sexually as of one who wants others to believe he is.

The mall was almost empty. Some members of the press, including local television crews, gathered inside the Whiteheadquarters. Uncertain of my role, I stood with a handful of curiosity seekers nearby, out on the concourse, keeping a watchful eye for assassins.

In his remarks, Whitehead hit on the themes he had stressed so far in his campaign — economic growth, job creation, and crime control. When he finished, the first thing the press wanted to know was whether his presence there meant that he and Roger Worthington had struck a deal.

"As governor I'll work to remove barriers for those who share my belief in progress," he said, adding that the "decent, honest, hard-workin' folks who toil in the factories and fields, coal mines and classrooms of Downstate Illinois deserve nothing less."

I doubted that Whitehead had ever dropped an ending g in his life and took his doing so then as a sign of desperation in the face of those stubborn poll numbers.

"Progress may cost," he said, "but stagnation exacts a *price* we can't afford."

His people smirked at the play on his opponent's name. Alice walked off with her shopping bag, squawking to herself and shaking her poor mad head.

The questions and answers went on for a few more minutes, then someone remembered the death threats and asked if he had received any recently.

"Thankfully, no," he said. Then, with his left hand clutching a lapel and the index finger of his right hand raised, he added, "But such threats won't keep Joe Whitehead from speaking his mind or from engaging in the democratic process."

Perhaps he calculated that if he referred to himself in the third person any would-be assassin wouldn't know who to shoot.

I have found it hard ever since to resist thinking that what happened next was God's way of wagging a finger in Joe Whitehead's face.

In such quick succession as to be almost simultaneous, three loud popping noises came from the street outside the north entrance, glass shattered, a voice cried out in pain, and a car squealed its tires and sped off.

I hit the floor and flattened. Everyone else out on the concourse did the same or scrambled for cover. Whitehead and the others in his headquarters ducked behind furniture and equipment. I looked up to see a young black male stagger through the first set of doors and collapse at the second set. I got to my feet and went to him. He was conscious, writhing in pain, and swearing revenge.

He had been shot in the left thigh. Another bullet had gone through the glass in two sets of doors above head level. By the time we all collected our breath and dusted ourselves off, the cops and an ambulance were on the scene.

After the ambulance left with the shooting victim, the cops hung around and asked some questions, but no one had seen enough to enlighten them. Joe Whitehead, visibly shaken, was escorted by his people to Lincoln Inn, where he stayed overnight.

In ensuing days, the shooter wasn't caught, but the cops learned that the victim was a member of one of two rival gangs, both of them offshoots from Chicago.

Coincidental though it was, the shooting brought my thinking back to the threats Whitehead claimed to have got and to that note I was carrying around. In my apartment that night, I pulled it out and re-read it.

WHITEHEAD WILL DIE HERE

I still thought it likely that Whitehead's camp had cooked up the story of his having received death threats. At the same time, I didn't buy what Art said about the note being a hoax, in part because I questioned Art's motives for pushing that idea. And then a word jumped off the page and hit me between the eyes: HERE. That made the threat place-specific, and its appearing after Whitehead announced his intention to locate at Lincoln Court suggested a link to that choice.

The likeliest link was the rumored deal between Whitehead and Worthington over the transformation of Lincoln Court into something much larger. Rumored or not, that transformation was already drawing opposition — from Lincoln Court's owners, according to those same rumors, and from residents of the nearby neighborhood that it threatened to displace. If there were such a link, then even if Whitehead had made up threats against his life, the note could be serious. It occurred to me that whoever left it with Art had most likely intended it to become public to make Whitehead rethink any inclination to support Worthington's plans if he was elected governor.

All of which left me in a curious position. If I kept the note secret, I could be putting Whitehead's life in danger. Yet for reasons I never got around to articulating to myself, that was what I did.

In the next few weeks, Whitehead came often, spending his nights in town at Lincoln Inn. Those at the mall who made it their business to pronounce on such matters assumed that Whitehead had his way with some of the young women who worked for him, despite, or because of, his being married. (Suzy Whitehead, all makeup and hairspray, showed up only once that I knew of, not in the company of her husband.)

Assassination talk pretty much faded. My guess was that Whitehead could see that he wasn't getting any traction from it and gave it up. As far as I knew, no follow-up death threats showed up in Art's office. I considered planting one myself to see if he would pass it on to me.

By late September it was clear that Whitehead's move to Lincoln Court had helped neither him nor the mall. In spite of having all but promised voters that he would increase their life spans, he still trailed in the polls by about ten points. Two more small retailers and an insurance agency in the basement vacated after his arrival. To save nickels, Art cut back on maintenance, to the detriment of appearances inside and out. The plywood that replaced the windows that had been shot out remained in place. The reigning question around the mall became not, as usual for that time of year, how lustily shoppers would spend money in the upcoming holiday season, but whether the place would even last until Thanksgiving.

The only remaining glimmer of hope, it seemed, was in Roger Worthington's long-rumored plans. But that hope rested on some tenuous assumptions: that the Parish family would be willing to sell; that Whitehead and Worthington had made some kind of deal; that Whitehead would get elected, which the polls suggested was unlikely. And it looked unlikelier when his opponent got endorsements from one newspaper after another, including the *Champaign News-Gazette*, which called Whitehead's professed solicitude for Downstate "cynical, transparent election-year posturing" given his voting record as a state senator.

When Whitehead came in the middle of October to appear at the Urbana Chamber of Commerce fall banquet, his smile was forced, his voice cracked, and the bags under his eyes had bags under them.

On the afternoon before the banquet, Whitehead held court for the press at his headquarters. Again, he stressed the need for Illinois and its leaders to foster a climate conducive to growth. Economic vitality, he assured us, benefits everyone, even those it might displace.

Roger Worthington was to be the featured speaker at the banquet that night. For days he had been dropping broad hints that he would use the occasion to unveil his plans for Lincoln Court. The pointedness of Whitehead's remarks suggested that he was backing those plans.

"It sounds like the deal's been done," one press guy shouted.

Whitehead delivered a non-committal reply through a tantalizing smile.

CHAPTER 6
THE DEVELOPER

I am not now nor have I ever been a member of the Communist Party. But the bumptious brand of capitalism practiced by guys like Roger Worthington helps me to understand Communists with genuine ideological motives.

It's probably unfair and reductive to attribute Worthington's fierce competitive drive to compensation for his standing five-feet-four in his wingtips, but one sensed that beneath all the bluff and bluster was a man desperate to be taken seriously. An old-school cigar chomper, through the 1960s and early 1970s he had built a thriving construction business, based in Urbana, on a reputation for bringing projects in on time and under budget. That was in part because he ran a non-union operation and brooked no complaints from those who worked for him.

I knew this firsthand. After coming to college, I worked one summer as a general helper and flunky on one of his crews building apartments near campus. He showed up one oppressively hot and humid day in August to find that a foreman had given us an extra five-minute break. He fired the guy on the spot, then broke his jaw with a right hook when he called Worthington a bastard.

To his credit, he was willing to do any work he asked his employees to do; he might show up at a site in good clothes, peel off his jacket, loosen his tie, roll up his sleeves, and weigh in with shovel and wheelbarrow.

Yet his accomplishments never quite matched the size and scale of those of his competitors. I used to hear from Beth, who was assigned by her law firm to be his legal counsel, that he often complained that the movers and shakers in the area, especially in Champaign, conspired against him. He might have been right, but I always felt that there was something else to it, that Worthington was the guy you excluded from the club for no other reason than that he so desperately wanted to join.

After he was shut out of contracts from the development of Prairieview Shopping Center in the early 1970s, he started vowing that, someday, somehow, he'd show those Champaign people a thing or two. But for years he was noncommittal about where and how he might do that.

Then in 1981 he moved his headquarters to an office suite that became vacant above the south concourse in Lincoln Court. The ostensible reason was the good deal he got on rent thanks to the mall's increasingly straitened circumstances. But many assumed the move was tied to his rumored intention to use Lincoln Court to stake his claim to being one of the big boys. By the summer of 1986, with the mall failing fast, he began hinting that he was about ready to show his hand. In the days leading up to the Chamber of Commerce's fall banquet, to be held at Lincoln Inn's Vandalia Room, he boasted that he'd surprise even those who had indulged in the wildest speculation.

The Inn handled its own security separately from the mall's. In this case, though, with Whitehead announcing he'd be in attendance and hostile rhetoric already emerging from neighborhood groups opposed to Worthington's plans, whatever they might be, Inn management put the finger on Art for an extra body. The schedule had Wendell Sollars, a farmer from near town who moonlighted with security, on duty at the mall. Bill Brazelton was assigned to the banquet. Brazelton was a spindle-legged endomorph who had hired on after getting booted from the Urbana police force for misconduct.

Through a permanently puzzled scowl, he seemed ever to be trying to figure out why he was so angry and belligerent. Around me, he acted like he had found the answer.

I was in the break room a few days before the banquet when he came in and checked the schedule and grumbled that he had planned to play poker that night. I offered to cover for him. I had several motives, none of which I shared: I was curious to see what Worthington was up to and thought I might as well get paid to do so; with that death threat against Whitehead in the breast pocket of my sport coat, I felt a kind of limited responsibility for his welfare; and it pleased me to heap the burning coals of kindness on Brazelton's head. He scowled and asked what I wanted in return. "Not a thing," I said. He told me not to hold my breath until he did the same for me and stomped off. I marked the change on the schedule.

The banquet was to begin at six-thirty, the program an hour later. Around two-thirty I began a late, peripatetic, two-course lunch — a pot of baked beans, a bowl of chili, and coffee at Steak 'n' Shake, followed by a fiery helping of kimchi, washed down by beer, at Seoul Food, a Korean restaurant in Campustown. After a nap back in my apartment, I walked down Green Street through the fine October early evening to the mall.

I checked in with Wendell to let him know where he could find me, then went to the Inn and slipped quietly through a rear service door into the Vandalia Room as waiters were serving dessert. I stood against a back wall.

Banqueters sat around tables with cotton tablecloths and flower-and-candle centerpieces. Beth and Steve Childress were near the front. Worthington was among those at a long table on the dais, in the center of which was a lectern with a microphone. Joe Whitehead sat at one end of that table.

After waiters cleared the dessert dishes and served coffee and cocktails, Chamber President Jessica Wong went to the lectern and awarded a plaque for something or other to some mug who stayed and prattled on about the wisdom of yearly upgrades of liability insurance. When he sat, she got back up to introduce Roger Worthington. Her eyebrows rising in anticipation, she let us know that we were about to witness the unveiling of a radical vision of Lincoln Court's, indeed Urbana's, retail future.

Worthington came to the lectern. I'm afraid this sounds like a cliché, but a hush came over the room. Worthington made the most of it. His thanks and acknowledgements seemed designed to test how long we could hold our breath. He walked to the end of the dais, stepped down, and came around front and center. Jessica Wong unclipped the microphone and handed it down to him. Worthington signaled to the wings.

Two young women in slit skirts entered through some curtains on the right, one pushing and one pulling a large, wheeled cart. They left it next to Worthington and exited the way they had come in. On the cart an irregular shape was covered by a blue satin sheet with a gold border and the Worthington Enterprises emblem in gold stitching.

W

E

Again, Worthington milked the moment for suspense. With the microphone in one hand, he stood in front of the cart and enumerated the qualities that made "this great big land of ours" the best country in the world: the ability of some people to overcome odds and to think big and boldly and competitively. He praised men with vision, men who dared to dream, those who believed in progress, those who abetted them, even those who, lacking the will or the wherewithal to accomplish great things, had the good sense to get out of the way.

"Ladies and gentlemen," Worthington said, "Take a look at downtown Urbana's future." With a histrionic flourish, he pulled the sheet from off the cart. "Lincoln Center!"

Murmurs rippled through the room. Some in the back stood for a better view. Among them, at a table just in front of me, was a vibrant young pair with excellent teeth. His eyes got wide. She formed her mouth into an O.

With Jessica Wong's help, Worthington draped the sheet over the lectern, leaving the emblem visible.

On the cart was a scale model of what appeared to be a complex of buildings arrayed over several acres — towers at both ends of a single large enclosure, surrounded by an expansive parking lot and satellite buildings in a variety of shapes and sizes.

Worthington picked up a pointer from the cart and held it like a scepter.

"The life blood of this town — of any town — is retail," he said, "and the future of retail is the megamall. What you see before you is a multi-purpose development that will transform the city of Urbana into a regional commercial power center."

Using the pointer to direct our attention, Worthington expounded upon the plan's features: Lincoln Inn, refurbished and expanded to double its present capacity; ten-story office towers at both ends of the retail center; in that center, some two-hundred stores — upscale and specialty shops, restaurants, cut-rate discounters, name-brand outlets; three anchor department stores; a professionally supervised play area for children; for "that Main Street feel," street names for the concourses; a multiplex cinema, an ice skating rink, eighteen holes of miniature golf; and, at the central hub, a performing arts venue.

Complementing the mall proper would be a wide range of freestanding satellites — more restaurants and outlet stores, at least one motel, a discount superstore.

"Now for my favorite part." He tapped a conical roof with his pointer. "The Big Ten Hall of Fame, where you can take a break from shopping and see in one place the glorious history of Big Ten sports."

The guy at the table in front of me pumped a fist into the air. His companion looked with sweet indulgence at her sports guy.

There would be approximately eight thousand parking spaces, but no one need dread a long walk through a parking lot. Worthington reached under the cart and brought up a model of what looked like a small bus.

"Shuttles, ladies and gentlemen, free of charge and running at frequent intervals."

Lincoln Center would attract not only shoppers, he assured us, it would attract tourists. "Millions of people live within a three-hour drive, many of whom will be willing to make that drive to the Lincoln Center I envision.

"How will this benefit our town?" Worthington asked. "For starters, Lincoln Center will wipe out unemployment. And my studies show that it will generate double the national average in retail sales per square foot annually."

The boost in sales and property taxes would help fund Urbana's schools, library, parks, roads, and other infra-structure, with plenty left over.

Were we concerned that the Champaign-Urbana metropolitan area might not be able to support two major malls?

"Maybe it can't," he said. He shook his pointer vaguely west. "For ten years Lincoln Court and Urbana have been losing business to the mall in Champaign. For ten years we've been hearing that we're one big community, that what's good for Champaign is good for the whole area. I say it's time we find out if the reverse is true, that what's good for Urbana is good for the whole area. Maybe it's time to see if that other retail complex down the road can survive some competition."

He assured downtown Urbana merchants that they had nothing to fear. "This won't replace downtown," he said. "This will *be* downtown, a downtown where you can practice your trade in a safe, enclosed, climate-controlled environment, *if* you get on board now."

He noted that he would be off in a few days to the International Council of Shopping Centers convention in Las Vegas, where he expected to be lining up some big-name tenants.

"Come and see me before I leave if you don't want to be left out in the cold."

Of course all this would cost money, lots of it. But he was certain of financial backing from a consortium of investors, some of whom had already made commitments. He was confident, too, of matching funds from the state and federal governments.

"I'd always prefer to work with the good old American dollar," he said, "but you might as well know that there's even interest in this project from foreign investors."

With a sideways glance at Whitehead, he expressed confidence that the next governor of Illinois would possess the vision to see the benefits of this project, not only to Urbana but to the entire state, and have the good sense to support it.

He paused, set his jaw, and scanned the room.

"Most of you here know Roger Worthington," he said, "and you know that Roger Worthington would never ask anyone to take a risk that he isn't willing to take himself. I'm putting *my* money, *my* reputation, *my very life* into this dream."

With his pointer he smacked the emblem on the sheet draped over the lectern.

"Those letters stand for more than Worthington Enterprises. Those letters spell *WE*. That's you and me, the hard-working people of Urbana. Together *we* can compete with anybody. Together *we* can transform this town into a retail power center."

He took a deep breath, swelling his chest, and almost shouted:

"Big dreams made this country great. Big dreams will keep it great. Are you ready to dream big with Roger Worthington?"

The couple in front of me were. They looked at each other and touched hands across the table, the candle flame reflecting in their eyes. I wouldn't have been surprised if they broke into song.

Worthington was finished. He handed the microphone back up and stood beaming next to his model. Jessica Wong went to the lectern. She looked officially excited. After urging us to think hard about what we had just seen and heard, she wished us all a good evening.

One by one, the banqueters rose. A few approached Worthington with purpose in their stride, but many held back, regarding each other tentatively, almost with embarrassment, as if still unconvinced but reluctant to be the only doubter. Whitehead began working the crowd.

I checked my watch. Wendell would be closing up shop soon and could use help. Instead of going out the way I had come in, I cut across the room to return to the mall through the hotel lobby.

By then, as I had hoped they would, the beans, chili, beer, and kimchi had worked their rank alchemy in my system, and as I wove my way through the cream of the community — expensively perfumed, cologned, and coiffed, dressed to the nines — I squeezed off silent, sulfurous advertisements for my lunch.

CHAPTER 7
COLD WATER

In a glass-enclosed case on a wall just inside the mall's east entrance, two large aerial photos showed the city block occupied by Lincoln Inn and Lincoln Court. In the first, taken in 1961, Lincoln Inn sat amid a mixed business and residential district. The other, taken three years later, after Lincoln Court, attached to the Inn, had opened as the first enclosed mall in Downstate Illinois, showed the Inn and Court and surrounding parking lots occupying the entire block.

On the Sunday morning after the banquet, I stood before those photos and tried to imagine an overlay of Worthington's project. His model and his remarks indicated that he wanted to expand to the south. In doing so he would wipe out scores of residences and small businesses, including Yen Ching, from which I often ordered takeout while on the job. To pull it off, Worthington would need a combination of luck, political clout, and plenty of financial backing. He would also need a fair amount of audacity, but of that he had no lack. Standing before those photos, I realized that in, say, five years, if everything fell into place, his model and his blueprints might be a reality on the ground.

Due perhaps to deadline restrictions, that day's *News-Gazette* carried not a word about the banquet. On Monday, this headline ran across two columns on page seven:

DEVELOPER PROPOSES
LINCOLN COURT MAKEOVER

The story under it was short and sketchy and didn't come close to conveying the scale of Worthington's plans. It occurred to me that that might have been a calculated oversight that represented the *News-Gazette*'s editorial policy.

In the next several days the paper addressed the matter in the form of letters to the editor, some op-ed pieces, and an editorial. Taken together, they confirmed my hunch.

The letters were mixed, with those opposed to the project outnumbering those in favor by about two to one. The other pieces amounted to brusque dismissal, pointing out what their authors felt were inconsistencies, exaggerations, bad math, insensitivity, and outright deceptions contained in Worthington's plans.

The most stinging attack came in an op-ed piece by Bruce Tomlinson, a U of I professor of urban studies. In it he challenged almost all of Worthington's claims for Lincoln Center. He argued that, in an area "already overbuilt for retail," Lincoln Center would only divide the pie into smaller pieces; that such projects have proven at best to be "flimsy anchors" for local economies, siphoning money that would be better spent on rehabbing depressed neighborhoods; that most of the jobs created by Worthington's project would be "menial, minimum-wage service jobs with few or no benefits."

The *News-Gazette*'s editorial weighed in on behalf of residents of the nearby neighborhood. It noted that even those not displaced by the project would suffer the headaches of encroaching development. And, citing Reilly's Law of Retail Gravitation, which stated that people will gravitate to the largest place most easily reached, it pointed out that Lincoln Center wouldn't be any closer to the interstate and, thus, still wouldn't be that most easily reached place. "And if Prairieview expands," it went on, "it won't even be the largest. We commend the desire to reinvigorate downtown Urbana," the editorial concluded, "and would be pleased to support a sensible scheme for accomplishing that. But, clearly, this isn't it."

All this negative reaction dampened the hopes of those who worked at the mall that Worthington's plan might save their jobs — never mind that it was years from realization and their jobs might disappear within weeks. They were silly to harbor such hopes in the first place, according to Mary Cobb.

For more than twenty years Mary had pronounced on matters of greater and lesser importance from behind her cash resister in the Lincoln Inn gift shop; her specialty was disabusing fools of their illusions. In this case, she would have us know that the old woman who lived alone on the Inn's top floor and never emerged from her rooms, who was a member of the Parish family that owned the Inn and the Court — that that old woman and her family would never allow ground to be broken on a project such as Worthington's as long as she lived. Never mind how Mary Cobb knew. She was Mary Cobb and she knew.

If she was right, Worthington's actions were hard to fathom, any deals he made in Las Vegas downright foolhardy. Either he was privy to information no one else had, or he was trying to break the Parishes down by sheer force and persistence.

Of more interest to me were those three cryptic words in the *News-Gazette* editorial: "if Prairieview expands." They seemed to have slipped under the radar, for I detected no subsequent reference to them. But they suggested the presence of another potential land mine on Worthington's path to glory.

When Worthington returned from Las Vegas he let it be known that while there he had made handshake agreements with some big-name national retail franchises for positions in the new Lincoln Center. Of course he couldn't reveal their names until certain legal and procedural matters had been tended to. He repeated his call to

Urbana merchants to sign on while there was still time. And he shrugged off the negative press. In a story in the *News-Gazette*, he was quoted as calling Tomlinson a "pencil-head academic who never did an honest day's work in his life." In blustery talk around the mall, he attached the word pencil to lower down on the professor's anatomy.

Worthington put his model in a utility alcove of the balcony near his office, out of the way but available for public inspection. It didn't stay there long. When Art Ziemann got word of its presence, he marched upstairs and informed Worthington that he wouldn't be allowed to use space that he hadn't rented to promote a plan to expand the mall that the mall's management and ownership hadn't approved. The two of them ended up in a shouting match on the balcony.

A small knot of people that included me watched from below on the concourse. It was a fine and diverting bit of theater, and I couldn't help wishing they had cutlasses to do it up right.

Things settled down after that. Art hid out in his office. Worthington put his model in storage, but busily jawboned and lobbied for support of his project. Joe Whitehead came and went often.

By election eve, Whitehead had narrowed the gap in the polls to about seven points, still outside the margin of error. Victory for Price looked certain. So did the probability that, lacking support from Springfield, Roger Worthington might never break ground on Lincoln Center, even if he could overcome all other obstacles. Still, he vowed that when Lincoln Center was in place Art would be lucky to find a job there selling shoes.

CHAPTER 8
THE HAND OF GOD

Leo slammed his newspaper shut, folded it roughly, and smacked it down on the table, rattling our coffee cups.

"I want a recount," he said.

"I expect Price does, too," I said. "Maybe he'll ask for one. Not that it will do any good."

"Are we supposed to accept that we're stuck with this nitwit for at least the next four years because of freaky weather?"

"Accept it or don't," I said. "It won't make any difference."

Late on election eve an unseasonably early ice storm moved into northeastern Illinois. It mostly missed the Republican collar counties and suburban Cook and dumped with a vengeance on Democratic Chicago, holding down turnout there. Downstate split about even. Joe Whitehead, who had awakened the morning of the election with little prospect of winning, awakened the next with a champagne hangover (or so I imagined) and a 7,000 vote margin of victory, virtually all of it coming from the suburbs. In post-election remarks, an unidentified member of Whitehead's campaign team suggested that that ice storm had been directed by the hand of God.

"The bum didn't have a chance," Leo said, "and now he's in the governor's mansion."

"Not yet," I said. "Lots could happen before he's sworn in. Maybe those death threats were for real after all and whoever made them backed off because Whitehead looked unlikely to win, but now that he has..." I finished the thought with a suggestive arch of my eyebrows.

Among some of the merchants, post-election buzz had Whitehead showing up any day to stand shoulder to shoulder with Worthington as the latter announced when ground was to be broken on the new Lincoln Center.

In the next few days, however, events transpired on several fronts that threatened to scuttle Worthington's project at least for the foreseeable future, and maybe for good.

First, on the Friday after the election, Illini Savings and Loan, which Worthington had identified as a backer, announced that it faced the prospect of having to write off $20 million worth of bad loans in Brazil.

The next day, a neighborhood group of about seventy-five people, concerned that Whitehead's victory would give Worthington the backing he needed in Springfield, staged a protest march through Lincoln Court, carrying handmade posters. They stopped under Worthington's office and shouted their determination to save their neighborhood from his bulldozers. Worthington watched through a window.

Art came up from the basement. He glowered at the protestors and threatened to have them removed by force if necessary. I stood around hoping that I wasn't the force he had in mind. Before Art made good on his threat, the protestors began to march out through the south doors, posters high, chanting all the way: "Hey Roger Worthington, leave our neighborhood alone."

Wincing at the off-rhyme, I watched as Worthington came onto the walkway outside his office. He took the butt end of a lit cigar from his mouth and, with index finger and thumb, flicked it in a long looping arc toward the demonstrators, who were jammed up at the exit, an easy target. The cigar butt hit a guy in the back of the head.

He turned, looked down at the butt then up at Worthington with rage on his face, shook his fist and shouted, "Over my dead body." Worthington answered with a middle-finger salute. On the terrace, Leo almost fell out of his chair laughing.

Then on the following Monday, the *News-Gazette* carried this front-page headline:

PRAIRIEVIEW TO EXPAND

According to the story, plans were in the works to double its retail square footage, add more restaurants and food court space, increase the number of its movie screens from four to twelve. It would add a Speier's department store, which had been considering the proposed new Lincoln Center, but which now deemed the prospects for that endeavor "too tenuous." A variety of satellite stores would go on the surrounding land, some of which had already been purchased by Prairieview's owners. The story ended by noting that financing was secured and that the prospects were good for whatever state-level support was needed, *thanks to the backing of governor-elect Joe Whitehead* (emphasis mine).

The *News-Gazette*, which had editorialized against Worthington's ambitions so recently, editorialized a couple of days later in favor of the Prairieview expansion. In a jab aimed straight at Worthington, it expressed the belief that it would accomplish everything "a certain other developer claims for his project, only without the rhetoric of community divisiveness and where it makes more sense, where Interstates 57 and 74 intersect, that 'most easily reached place.'"

Worthington was livid. He marched around with murder in his eyes, clenching and unclenching his fists. He huffed, fumed, and fulminated, calling Whitehead a liar and vowing to show him the next time he came around what happened to someone who betrays Roger Worthington.

A spokesman for Whitehead tried to put the best face on things. He explained that, indeed, Whitehead had committed himself to Roger Worthington and his plan, but that nothing in their agreement prevented him from supporting the Prairieview project as well. "The governor-elect," he said, "didn't see why both projects couldn't go forward."

My calculation was that what the spokesman said was part truth and part disingenuous flummery. I doubted that Whitehead believed that two such projects could proceed simultaneously in the same area, competing for scarce money, political capital, and other resources. But I didn't doubt that Whitehead had expressed his support discreetly to both parties — before the election, when he was going around begging for campaign contributions.

When word got around that Whitehead would come to Urbana on the day after Thanksgiving to make an important announcement, busybodies at Lincoln Court licked their chops over the prospect of a donnybrook between him and Worthington if he showed up at the mall.

CHAPTER 9
BLACK FRIDAY

Every year on the day after Thanksgiving, Black Friday as it has since become known, Lincoln Court held a mall-wide sale. That year it was viewed by the merchants not as the official kickoff to the holiday shopping season, but rather as an opportunity to clear out inventory before the place went belly up. However the customers thought of it, they showed up in such numbers that someone unfamiliar with the circumstances might have mistaken Lincoln Court for a robust retail environment. To those of us who knew better, they were vultures come to pick the carcass clean.

Selected merchandise had been moved out onto to the concourses. Everything in Craddock's was on double-deep discount, and many of the other stores had followed its lead. At Craddock's outside entrance, an impatient rabble pressed against the doors before the time for opening came. I couldn't help but wonder about the safety of the young female clerk who had been assigned to unlock. When she did, only by quickly backing into the wedge of space behind the open door did she avoid being trampled.

As after the breaking of a dam water rushes headlong until it finds room to spread out, so the bargain-hungry mob dispersed into men's and women's clothing, housewares and linens, sporting goods, and footwear — a rabid, snarling bunch, taken all together, and it was the weakest to the wall. God help the register clerk who waited on someone out of turn. And I saw two women converge upon a garment at the same time and pull it in opposite directions until it ripped, there being no Solomon at hand to mediate. For one whose sensibility is properly attuned, it is possible to hear in that rip the fabric of civilization give way.

Around three o'clock I spotted the governor-elect, unaccompanied, sneak in through the north entry in trench coat with upturned collar, sunglasses, and, it seemed, hiding under a wide-brimmed hat. He slipped into his headquarters for a few minutes — Art had granted Whitehead a short-term lease but squeezed him for rent for the entire month of November — then right back out again. Clearly, he wanted to go unnoticed, and for all I could see he pulled it off. (It turned out that he had come to town to announce his appointment of a U of I business school dean to his cabinet.)

By eight-thirty that night, with half an hour left until closing, the place had mostly cleared out. Weary clerks and store managers visited on the concourses to compare notes and to begin pulling merchandise back in.

I was browsing the leavings of the bargain table in front of Schwartz's bookstore when I heard what sounded like the breaking of a window overhead. I looked up.

Glass rained down. Forty feet above the concourse a man hung for a second or two with his leg hooked at the knee on a piece of the framework of the fenestrated vault, then fell and landed with a sickening thud about twenty feet from where I stood. For a moment, the only sound was of the machinery on the roof of the hotel, audible through the broken glass. Then a woman screamed.

I put down the book I had been skimming and approached. He had landed bottom up, his face turned away from me, dressed in only a pair of red silk boxer shorts. Blood ran from under his hair. I walked around for a better look.

It was Joe Whitehead. I bent down and felt on his neck for a pulse. He didn't have one.

CHAPTER 10
I, WITNESS

On the inside of a semicircle formed by some uniformed cops and me, UPD Chief Detective Harold Bivins squatted on his heels next to the body of Joe Whitehead. He stood, broken glass crunching under his feet, hitched his pants, shook his head, and sighed with exasperation.

"I saw him fall," I said.

He turned to me. "What's that?" He seemed as much annoyed as curious.

"I was standing right over there, just outside the bookstore, when I heard the glass break. I looked up to see him hanging by one leg for a second or two, then down he came." I gave him my name and told him I was with mall security.

Bivins looked me up and down and wrinkled his nose.

"You see anything else?"

"No."

I realized as I spoke, though, that something else was lodged in my subconscious that I couldn't get to.

A uniformed cop came to tell Bivins that he had learned that Whitehead had been staying in room 637 of Lincoln Inn. Bivins left a couple of cops with the body and took some others with him to the Inn desk to get a key to Whitehead's room. I tagged along.

We rode up on the elevator. When we got off we went down a hall, turned and went down another hall to room 637. The door was slightly ajar, with the latch bolt resting against the strike plate. Bivins pushed it open warily and led the way into the room.

Lying on the nearest of the two beds was a young woman with shoulder-length black hair. She was covered to mid-thigh by a sheet and dressed in only a tank top. A cop whistled a long, appreciative note.

Bivins went to her. With a sour look at the cop who had whistled, he pulled the sheet up to her chin. He opened one of her eyelids and put two fingers on her wrist.

"She's alive, but barely," he said. "Fergie, go back down. When the ambulance comes, send the paramedics up here."

As we waited, he and the other cops looked around. I went to a door at the far end of the room and through it onto a balcony. Directly below was the glass Whitehead had fallen through. Bivins came out and joined me. We could see the cops and the body. The flashing lights from the cop cars outside the nearest entry lent a surreal effect to the scene. We went back in the room.

In a short time, paramedics came in with a bed on wheels. They took the young woman out. Bivins gave one cop instructions to stay there until an evidence team came up. He and I and the other cops went out and waited for the elevator then went down.

Members of the press had arrived and were at work with cameras, notebooks, and hand-held tape recorders. A police photographer took pictures of Joe Whitehead. A gaggle of curious shopkeepers watched from behind the crime scene tape that had been strung up, tisking and frowning and craning their necks and speaking out of the sides of their mouths to each other. Knowing them as I did, I knew that they had already set the rumor mill to cranking.

Art Ziemann showed up and ducked under the tape. Bivins apprised him of the situation and told him that the mall would have to be closed for the night. By then it was five minutes to closing time anyway, so Art didn't squawk. But he pointed out that the crime scene, strictly speaking, assuming a crime had been committed, was apparently Lincoln Inn and not Lincoln Court, and that he could see no reason why the mall should not open on time the next day for business as usual.

Bivins shrugged. Who was he to oppose the march of commerce?

The young woman, her breathing shallow and her heartbeat weak, was taken away in the ambulance that had come for Whitehead. He was taken later in a second ambulance, a footnote to the political history of Illinois: the man who was elected governor but who never served a day.

The merchants blamed dismal sales the rest of that weekend on the chilling effect of his death, and took it for a portent that the end was ineluctably at hand.

CHAPTER 11
THE DEAL

Call me morbid, but when I returned to my apartment in Campustown on the night Whitehead died, I sat for a long time in my bay window, four floors above Green Street, imagining Whitehead conscious as he fell, even though for some reason I suspected he hadn't been, so that I could imagine the thoughts racing through his head as he plummeted to a certain and hideous death.

First to mind was chagrin that he'd never be governor after all, never use the office to attract bribes and women. Then again, I've heard that people in extreme situations focus on some pretty trivial things, so on his way down he might have noticed the oddly posed mannequins in Craddock's display window or heard the Muzak version of Christmas music that was playing. After a while, though, I worked on trying to shake loose whatever it was that had registered below the conscious level when I saw Whitehead fall. It wouldn't come.

It wasn't the rowdy Friday night I was used to witnessing from up there, the students having cleared out for Thanksgiving, so I was able to think in relative quiet. Over and over, I saw Whitehead hanging by one leg through the broken window, then falling, then landing with a sickening thud. And two other images came to mind — Worthington's caterwauling over Whitehead's supposed betrayal of him, and something I had seen after the Chamber of Commerce banquet.

While helping close and lock the mall that night, I spotted Worthington, Whitehead, and Beth go upstairs together to Worthington's office suite. The light in his conference room went on. They stayed for about an hour. Except for its reinforcing my cynicism about business people and politicians scratching each other's backs, I didn't think much of that meeting at the time. But in those sleepless hours in my bay window on the night Whitehead died, it began to take on significance. The obvious conclusion was that Worthington and Whitehead had struck a deal and that when Worthington thought he'd been betrayed he either killed Whitehead or had him killed. Before coming to that conclusion, though, I'd need to know what was said in that meeting. As it happened, I thought there might be some chance that I could find out.

Worthington's suite comprised three rooms in tandem. His receptionist worked in one; another held drafting and layout tables; the third was the conference room in which that meeting had taken place after the banquet. For years, Beth had served as Worthington's legal counsel on behalf of the law firm she worked for. Often, in response to her request that I "be a dear," I would deliver sandwiches and coffee to her and Worthington and clients during working lunches, so I was familiar with the layout. And it was Beth who let me in on the fact that Worthington often recorded conversations in his conference room on a reel-to-reel tape recorder under the bar, virtually always without his guests' knowledge.

On the day after Whitehead died, I was scheduled to work from early afternoon to closing time. When the place had cleared out, I went up to the monitor room, which adjoined Worthington's conference room in an L-shaped arrangement at the end of the walkway. With regard to security, the monitors were of little value, but with the screens off the room was cool, dark, and quiet, and I sometimes went there while on duty to relax and recharge by lying on the carpeted floor in *savasana* for ten or fifteen minutes. None of my keys would have got me into Worthington's conference room, but there was enough space between the door and the frame and enough play in the simple latch bolt that I was able to wedge my way in with the blade of my pocket knife. Snooping around with a penlight, I found the taping system behind the bar. I plugged in and put on a set of headphones, sat on the floor and set to playing the tape already on the reels.

What I heard didn't sound like what I was after. I reversed and tried again. There was Worthington's voice, then Whitehead's, then Worthington's again. I reversed and played several times until I heard the clink of ice cubes in a glass and the beginning of what I suspected was the conversation that took place after the banquet.

Worthington spoke first: "How goes the campaign, Joe?"

Whitehead: "It goes. The poll numbers are stubborn, but... What I need now is money for TV time Downstate."

Worthington didn't answer. A politician in need of cash is a manipulable thing, and I imagined his savoring the moment as he puffed on a cigar and watched Whitehead squirm.

Beth broke the silence: "How much money?"

Whitehead cleared his throat. I tried to imagine his thinking at that moment: Ask for less than he could have got, and he'd waste his opportunity and look like a fool; ask for too much and he'd increase his chance of getting nothing. He finally answered: "Plenty. My people have the numbers, but I know it's well into six figures. I've got other sources, and I won't ask for that much, but whatever you could spare will help. Let's say five figures, and the higher the better."

Worthington: "That's a hell of a lot of money."

Whitehead: "I know, but... [The next few words were garbled.]... compared to what that project of yours will be worth to you once it's in place."

Worthington: "What's your point?"

Whitehead: "My point is that you and I both know how many boards and commissions have to put their stamp of approval on the kind of thing you have in mind. Whoever's governor of this state will have a say over who sits on those boards and commissions and the decisions they make."

Worthington: "Are you saying that if I don't float you five figures and you're elected you'll see to it that Lincoln Center doesn't get built?"

Whitehead: "Not at all. I'm saying that those who help me get over the top will have someone in the governor's mansion who takes care of his friends, and you can be one of them."

Beth: "Suppose we give you all that money and you lose the election?"

Whitehead: "That could happen, and it makes it a gamble on your part. I'd still be in the Senate, though, and a player in Springfield. But I don't plan to lose."

Worthington: "I imagine Price would say the same."

Whitehead: "I'm sure he would, and one of us will be right. I happen to think that's going to be me, especially if I get the backing I need for a big push Downstate. I've got hotshots from Chicago working on these ads, with orders to go for the jugular."

A silence ensued. Finally, Worthington spoke: "I'll sleep on it. One way or another you'll know my answer by Monday. If it's yes, you'll see money coming in, plenty of it and fast."

Whitehead started to speak, but Worthington cut him off: "Now let me be clear. If I *do* invest some tens of thousands of dollars in you, and if you *do* get elected, and if then you *don't* come through for me... I'll just say this — I don't forget, and I don't forgive."

Beth added something at that point that I couldn't pick up; it was covered by the sound of a door opening and another layer of voices, Beth's and Worthington's. They weren't coming from the tape.

The light came on in the room. I stayed on the floor and quietly toggled the tape off. Despite the headphones still covering my ears, I heard Beth's voice from the adjoining room:

"I don't have time for drinks. Let's just do this."

The light went out and the door closed. I took off the headphones. In a crouch, I came out from behind the bar and got up next to the door that had opened.

I heard papers fall to the floor, a vague rustling and bumping about, the clunk of shoes, what might have been a zipper, then Worthington saying in a growly whisper, "Come to papa, baby."

There followed about thirty seconds of grunting and huffing, all of it Worthington's, at the end of which he gave out a long, throaty exhalation.

"Get up," Beth said. "I've got work to do."

As they made themselves presentable, Beth admonished Worthington that he'd be smart to avoid expressing his satisfaction over Whitehead's demise quite as openly as he had in the past twenty-four hours.

"That son-of-a-bitch betrayed me!" Worthington shot back.

"Maybe so," Beth said, "but if you get people to thinking you killed Whitehead or had him killed, then you risk undermining yourself at a time when things might be falling into place. You'll be interested to know that I took the liberty of getting in touch with Charlotte Parish and that she and her brother may be ready to deal. I wasn't going to say anything yet because I wasn't sure you'd want me acting on my own."

Worthington's voice was hot with urgency. "When? What did she say? Give it to me word for word."

"Recently. Very recently. Her exact words don't matter. The main point is that she sounded at least ready to listen to an offer. If she is, and if the people at Kitsu are serious about backing you, then you need a cool head right now, and the coolest one you've got is mine. You'd be smart to tone down the talk about Whitehead and to let me play hostess when Matsuta comes to look the place over."

"Exactly what I had in mind, my dear," Worthington said. "Use all your charms."

I'd heard enough. Stealthily, I returned to the monitor room. Standing back in the dark, I watched through the tinted window in the door that opened onto the balcony.

Beth emerged first. She touched her hair, smoothed and adjusted her skirt, then left. Worthington came out minutes later. He paused and looked over the railing at the empty mall, perhaps seeing his dream version in its place. He pulled a cigar from the inside of his suit coat, stuck it in his mouth, lit it with a match and walked off.

Come to papa?

CHAPTER 12
AN UNLIKELY PAIRING

It is an enduring mystery to me that Beth and I, who parted within ten years of vowing never this side of death to part, could have regressed by then to being mere casual acquaintances. Yet such was the case.

We both matriculated at the University of Illinois in the fall of 1965. I had come from poor, tiny Newman, a coal-mining town less than an hour's drive to the southeast; it might as well have been on the other side of the solar system for all it prepared me for the life and possibilities of a place like the U of I.

Newman kids didn't escape, as a rule, and I probably assumed I'd live and labor and die as had my father, who spent his working life under the ground in the employ of the Peabody Coal Company and succumbed to black lung disease at the age of thirty-nine, when I was fourteen. But a high school counselor saw more potential in me than I would have guessed was there and urged me to go to college, even helped me narrow my choices and fill out applications.

I moved into a residence hall on Florida Avenue, assigned to share a room with Marcus Paul, a jazz trumpeter from Belleville on a music scholarship. Marcus was a diminutive fellow with horn-rimmed glasses and a dismaying amount of nervous energy. He sang scat, slapped out beats on his legs or whatever surface was at hand, blew the trumpet and dope, my first exposure to drugs, with equal frenzy. For a college freshman, he had worldly ways that I can credit only to his immersion in the East St. Louis-area jazz scene in which he had been raised. By early October he had formed a band and was playing on campus and in clubs around town. I have no idea when he studied for classes. He insisted that I take in his gigs and, more largely, included me in his social circle.

By then the U of I, like many American college campuses, was rapidly coming to a rolling boil, what with civil rights and war protests, the burgeoning drug scene, the sexual revolution — all very heady stuff for a small-town boy like me. Perhaps because I was so blissfully ignorant of how out of my league I was, I got quickly swept up and carried along as if on a wave. I had come here short-haired, myopic and naive. By Thanksgiving, I was long-haired and unshaven, vocally anti-establishment, and had taken up smoking filterless Camels, the occasional joint, and drinking espresso laced with whiskey.

The circle of friends into which I fell included Beth, sophisticated and lovely, who had commenced her flirtation with the Bohemian lifestyle. I forget who made the first move or showed the first sign of interest but, somehow, we became a couple.

Ours was an unlikely pairing. I had grown up with a rusty Ford truck on blocks in the side yard; she had grown up with live-in servants, hell, with servants in the family's summer "cottage" in Harbor Springs, Michigan, the garage for which was finer than the house I was raised in. Never mind all that, though, it was the Sixties.

We were an item off and on, but mostly on, for the next few years and married late in 1968, in Urbana, in a brief secular ceremony without family present.

The next fall, with dual degrees in Marketing and Finance in hand, Beth entered the U of I law school. She breezed through then took a position as a specialist in real estate law with Blessing Harkey, and Stubbs, whose offices were on the basement level of Lincoln Court.

In the meantime, in stark contrast to Beth's focused drive, I had changed majors nearly a dozen times — from history, to political science, to math, to psychology, to philosophy, to journalism, to English, to geography, to cartography, to astronomy — dabbling at everything, completing nothing. There is a type of man — I seldom see this in women — that is temperamentally incapable of finishing things. At that time in my life I was one of that type. Eight years after entering college, by then married to Beth for the last five of them, I gave up pursuit of a degree for good, if I can be said ever to have pursued one. I was out of school and unemployed as Beth's salary approached six figures.

On my behalf and without my knowledge she made inquiries at Lincoln Court, may even have known someone in a position to pull strings, so that I might fill an opening that had come up with security there if I were so inclined. I had frequented the place enough to see that the job wouldn't demand a lot and that I'd be paid for not much more than walking around. Never mind that it paid minimum wage, I'd be minimally challenged, and that suited me. Beth joined me in pretending to believe that it would be a temporary placement until I found some better way to use my talents, whatever those might be, and make my mark in the world.

I realize now that people must have wondered how Beth, so bright and sharp and accomplished and rising so fast, could bear to be tethered to a loser like me, a part-time minimum-wager with no prospects for a degree or a profession. Beth must have wondered, too. But it simply never occurred to me that our connection might have been a source of shame or embarrassment to her or a drag on her ambitions.

In the meantime, by more or less unspoken agreement, we had remained childless, owing to Beth's use of birth-control pills. Then in the fall of 1978, she came down with what she thought was the flu; she was queasy and weak and spent her mornings vomiting.

When the symptoms persisted, she saw a doctor, who informed her that she was about one month pregnant. The pill had failed us.

Such was our pattern of communication by then that we didn't discuss our options or priorities. I guess it never occurred to me that we wouldn't have the baby, or, I realized later, to Beth that we would.

Her symptoms passed. We spoke in good humor of the little one knitting inside her, seemed, to me at least, to have arrived at tacit agreement to become parents.

Indeed, I found that I had developed a strong emotional investment in the prospect of becoming a father. Beth and I had been getting along poorly, and I hoped that parenthood might rejuvenate our marriage. (At the time we were at odds over the issue of travel. Beth felt that if one were to be taken seriously by people who mattered, one must experience at least Europe firsthand. "Travel is so *broadening*," a woman of our acquaintance liked to say, stretching the first syllable all the way to London, lest one miss the point. I dismissed the whole business as a chasing after wind, an attitude that Beth found incomprehensible.) In short, without fooling myself about the work and responsibility involved, I set about excitedly planning for life postpartum.

At my prompting, we had begun to consider names. One evening after work I shared with Beth a few I had come up with for both genders. At which point, without showing a hint that the news might shock or disappoint, she informed me that she was feeling under the weather, having that afternoon had the pregnancy aborted. Excuse her if she retired early without eating. I'd find leftovers in the fridge.

How to account for my response? Resilience? Shock? A desire to pay back her callousness in the same coin? Whichever was the case, without showing a hint of dismay or of concern for her condition, I made a cold meatloaf sandwich and a pot of coffee and ate while watching a pro basketball game.

In the weeks that followed, we might as well have been mere roommates, with nothing more in common than shared space. A month after the abortion, I came home to a note on the kitchen counter in Beth's hand informing me that she had left me for Steve Childress, a partner in her law firm who, presumably, had left his wife Cindy.

Steve was a hard-partying punk Republican of the kind one sees more often these days — power, money, rock 'n' roll — and had been on the fringe of our crowd in college. After law school he married Cindy, a hairsprayed suburban princess. Somehow we evolved into a foursome. We dined out and at each other's houses, went together to movies and bars. I drew the line at golf. As often as not, Beth and Steve talked shop, leaving Cindy and me to manage as best we could.

Beth ended the note by informing me that her lawyer would be in touch with my lawyer. It was a measure of either the distance we had grown apart or of Beth's self-absorption that we could be living under the same roof without her knowing that, except for being married to one, I didn't have a lawyer.

Sitting alone in the dark house that night, it occurred to me that I might not have fathered the child Beth aborted.

By the time we were ready to settle the terms of divorce, without quite articulating it to myself, I had decided on becoming a sort of secular monk, the fruit of some thinking that had taken root well before things went to smash. Beth showed up with Steve and a divorce specialist from within their firm; I came without benefit of legal counsel. They didn't see how we could proceed. I assured them we could.

The car? For years I had gone about mostly by bicycle and on foot. They were welcome to it. Our household possessions — furniture and appliances, TV, stereo? They would do me a favor by taking the entire lot. The house? We could afford it thanks only to

Beth's salary; it was all the same to me if she sold it or Steve moved in. (Both of them, it turned out, required more space.)

Steve was confused, Beth downright suspicious, but we did the deal. To this day they regard me warily.

I lived for a short time at the YMCA, then moved into the Campustown apartment I still occupy.

Cindy, after recovering from the betrayal and hurt, let me know that she'd be pleased to make the new arrangement symmetrical. Steve, as part of the settlement, had left her their Amway business, and she was prepared, even eager, to take me on as full partner and mate. Unkind me, I almost laughed out loud in her face. And yet...

Cindy was not unattractive, and her perky hair and clothes full of static electricity had at times taken on a kind of kinky appeal for me. More than once I had found myself curious about what might be under all that polyester. Did I actually consider her proposal? I wince now to think that I might have.

In the end, though, I did not — could not — allow myself to commit to a relationship with a woman so deadly serious about country club membership and direct marketing.

CHAPTER 13
TESTIMONY

On the Monday morning after Whitehead's death, I was walking rounds at the mall when someone behind me called my name. I stopped and turned. It was Harold Bivins, accompanied by a cop in uniform. He made a gesture intended to pin me to the spot and came my way.

"I wanted to call you, but you're not in the book," he said.

"I don't have a phone."

I believe he actually flinched. When he recovered, he said, "Can we talk? Are you free?"

I took in the virtually empty mall with a sweep of my hand.

"I might be able to give you five minutes," I said.

We went down to the Community Room and sat at a table. The other cop pulled out a small notepad and a pencil.

At Bivins's prompting, I repeated what I had told him over Whitehead's body on Friday night. As I spoke, I saw Whitehead fall in my mind's eye, and the thing that had been stuck in my subconscious shook loose and rolled free, like a lottery ball.

"He didn't scream," I said, "either before he hit the glass or after he crashed through and fell to the concourse. I could be wrong about before, but I don't think so. The first thing I heard was the glass breaking. I looked up to see him hanging from the framework for a second, then down he came. There was no sign of life and no scream."

Bivins looked to the cop taking notes to make sure he was getting it all down, then back at me. He rasped his hand across the stubble on his chin.

"Are you saying he was already dead?"

"Strictly speaking, no," I said. "Only that I don't think he was conscious as he fell."

"Anything else?"

"Yes, a couple of things. You probably noticed, but the door to Whitehead's room wasn't entirely shut when we got up there. I saw it before you went in. I was the last one in, and it didn't shut all the way behind me. I had to push it to get the latch to catch."

"I noticed," Bivins said. "We're talking to hotel staff about that. And?"

"Up in Whitehead's room, when we first went in, I noticed two parallel tracks in the nap of the carpet between the bed and the door to the balcony."

"Tracks."

"They looked like they could have been made by the heels of someone being dragged from under the arms. By the time we came in from the balcony they were more or less wiped out by all the tramping around."

If Bivins took that as criticism he showed no sign. In fact, he seemed to dismiss the matter as insignificant, maybe the only alternative to admitting that he hadn't sufficiently secured the scene against contamination of evidence.

"Okay," Bivins said. "I'd appreciate it if you kept your eyes and ears open. So far you're the closest thing we have to a witness. Being with security you're in a good position. Are you here every day?"

"Just about."

"Good. If you see or hear something you think might help, let me know."

He took the pad of paper from the cop, wrote on a sheet, tore it off and gave it to me.

"You can reach me at this number," he said. "Leave a message if I don't answer."

I put the sheet in the inside pocket of my sport coat with the one containing the death threat against Whitehead. For a brief moment I thought of pulling that out and presenting it to him but decided against it. I'd have had a hard time explaining why I hadn't told him about it sooner.

We were done. There was plenty else Bivins might have asked and I might have said. He mentioned neither the vitriol Worthington had been spewing in public over his belief that Whitehead had betrayed him nor Worthington's expressions of satisfaction, again in public, over Whitehead's death. Needless to say, I didn't tell of my breaking into Worthington's office and what I had learned there. In fact, I sensed in that interview with Bivins what I had sensed standing across from him over Whitehead's body, that what he wanted more than anything was for the case to go away.

Harold Bivins struck me as slow, myopic, and literal minded, and I couldn't help but speculate that his rise to the position of Chief Detective might be attributable less to acumen and expertise on his part than to the corruption scandal of a few years back that had cleared space above him.

At any rate, at least for the time being, I preferred to hold my cards close to the vest until I saw how the game played out. In the next couple of days information emerged that suggested it would play out in some intriguing ways.

The autopsy on Joe Whitehead showed that he had ingested booze and Seconal that night, probably enough in combination to knock him out, although not necessarily to kill him.

Martha Herrera, the young woman found in Whitehead's room at Lincoln Inn, had been taken in a coma to Carle Hospital in Champaign. Cops stood by her room in shifts, reportedly in the hope that if she regained consciousness she might tell of what had happened that night with Whitehead.

She never came out of the coma. Late Monday night her vital signs went flat, and all attempts to revive her failed.

The autopsy on her showed Seconal and booze in her system too, in addition to an over-the-counter antihistamine, and that she had been in the early stages of pregnancy, a combination that might have brought on the coma. The police, meanwhile, had learned that she had worked for the Downtowner Escort Service in Champaign, long rumored to be a front for prostitution.

Before she died, her mother and brother Victor came down from Chicago. As if her mother hadn't enough to fret over, her brother was jailed after trying to stab one of the cops standing guard after overhearing him refer to his sister as a whore while talking to the cop who had come to relieve him.

By mid-week the cops still hadn't arrested anyone and still hadn't used the word *murder*. Their daily briefings suggested that they might try to pass the affair off as an accidental overdose with separate lethal consequences. Their official speculation was that Whitehead, drugged and intoxicated, had wandered out to the balcony for some fresh air and fallen off.

Word traveled around the mall that someone in the Urbana Police Department had leaked that what the cops really believed, but either knew they couldn't prove or didn't dare make public because of the political fallout, was that Martha Herrera knew she was pregnant and had tried to convince Whitehead that he was the father, possibly with the intention of blackmailing him; that he had used the Seconal to try to shut her up for the moment until he found a way to shut her up for good, but in doing so had somehow got caught up in his own scheme.

I thought I detected a smokescreen. If the cops could convince the public that the only choices were either the official version they were floating or the leaked one, then they might successfully squelch talk of murder or assassination and thus defuse the political powder keg the case had the potential for becoming.

But I held my peace and did no more than what Bivins asked me to do. From the terrace, while consuming coffee and news — compulsively, voraciously, like a Yemeni his khat — and chewing the fat with Leo and Eddie and whoever else might stop by, I kept an eye out not only for retail theft and other petty crime, but also for anything that might shed light on the deaths of Joe Whitehead and his paramour.

CHAPTER 14
A THEORY, A SUSPECT,
AN ARREST

By the next Thursday, with the Urbana cops still in a muddle over whether Joe Whitehead and Martha Herrera had been the victims of foul play, Republicans all over the state were screaming bloody murder. Their screams were so loud, strident, and insistent that lame duck Republican governor George Foley asked the Illinois State Police's Division of Criminal Investigation to lend a hand.

The state team, led by DCI chief Ken Lakis, arrived on Friday afternoon and set up shop in the UPD headquarters, only a couple of blocks from Lincoln Court.

Lakis had a reputation in law enforcement circles for firing from the hip and asking questions later, if he asked them at all. In the past year or so he had been waging a war on organized crime that some characterized as brave, others as foolhardy, and that many considered to be in the service of political ambitions.

Lakis spent a couple of days nosing around the mall by himself or with other members of the DCI team. Once or twice I saw him with Bivins in tow. I expected to be summoned for questioning, but wasn't. To the surprise of a lot of people, word leaked that Lakis had confirmed Roger Worthington's alibi and dismissed him as a suspect. On late Sunday afternoon Lakis announced that the next morning he would hold a press conference.

Lakis came down the steps in front of the UPD headquarters on a wet, chilly Monday morning, dressed in a camel coat and a wide-brimmed hat. Television film crews and newspaper and radio reporters shivered at the bottom, their breath vaporizing in the air. I stood off to the side.

"Ladies and gentlemen," Lakis said, "early this morning Richie Miranda, a bellhop at Lincoln Inn, was arrested for the murder of governor-elect Joe Whitehead and" — he turned to an aide for clarification — "and Martha Herrera."

That, as far as I knew, was the first official use of the word *murder* in connection with the case.

Reporters pressed forward and shouted questions. Lakis held his hands up in a plea for patience.

"Please," he said, "let me background the case first."

He began by sketching the outlines of the civil war within the ranks of organized crime that had been raging in and around Chicago since spring and that more recently had begun to spill over into Downstate. As one long fascinated by the machinations of the mob, I had been following the story in the newspapers with some interest.

The war was precipitated when Chicago syndicate boss Vincent Castarelli had a debilitating stroke in February. He survived, but at his advanced age of seventy-six, it seemed unlikely that he would ever again run the business with his customary thoroughness and ruthlessness.

Castarelli had never groomed a successor, preferring to keep his subordinates' ambitions in check by playing them off against each other. The strategy worked as long as he was fit and in charge; with his life in the balance, the fight for the leadership became a free-for-all. After some bloody opening rounds, the main contenders that emerged were Jimmy "The Lip" Ayuna and Frankie Albert.

Ayuna had never got high marks from mob watchers for his intelligence, but his reputation for ruthlessness was exceptional even by mob standards, and he had a small but loyal following of young thugs. Albert was longer in the ranks and favored by those loyal to Castarelli.

The war took a toll on both sides. Yet for us Downstate, at least those of us curious enough to watch, it still had the feel of a spectator sport. Then in late summer the blood that had been washing the gutters of Cook County began to flow south.

From the perspective of a Downstate politician, the major highways on the road map of Illinois form a funnel that drains money to the northeast. Viewed with knowledge of the mob's involvement Downstate, those roads look like tentacles.

As Castarelli's lieutenants, Ayuna and Albert oversaw different operations but in overlapping territories. After the old man's stroke, each tried to muscle in on the other. For years, Albert had run a moderate-sized prostitution trade out of taverns and escort services in some of the larger Downstate towns. Ayuna tried cutting into Albert's trade by setting up business at rest stops and truck stops along the interstates near those towns.

On Labor Day weekend, having caught wind of Ayuna's incursion, Albert sent some goons to a rest stop along Interstate 57 north of Champaign, where they executed one of Ayuna's pimps. Lest that message not be emphatic enough, they then broke into a van and fired bullets into the brains of a prostitute and her john while they were transacting business.

That set off a series of retaliatory strikes in and around several towns, including Champaign and Urbana. When some civilians got caught in crossfires, decent folks expressed astonished outrage, and law enforcement agencies came under public pressure to take action. Politicians, especially those up for election, struck indignant poses and accused their opponents of being soft on crime. Joe Whitehead, behind in the polls and desperate for an issue to capitalize on, declared personal war on the mob, vowing if elected to eradicate it from the state of Illinois once and for all.

"Now," Lakis said, "you're probably wondering how all this relates to the murder of Joe Whitehead."

He asserted as fact what had long been rumored, that the Downtowner Escort Service, Martha Herrera's employer, was a front for prostitution, then added that it was part of Frankie Albert's operation. He said records obtained from The Downtowner under court order showed that Joe Whitehead had availed himself of Martha Herrera's services on four occasions since September, including on the night he died. Lakis had further learned that around six-thirty on that evening, Lincoln Inn room service had delivered some food and a pitcher of margaritas to Whitehead's room. Tests on the remains of the contents of the pitcher revealed that it had been heavily laced with Seconal. The room service order had been delivered by Richie Miranda, a student at the U of I who had started work at the Inn early the previous summer and who was — Lakis all but paused for a drum roll — the nephew of Jimmy "The Lip" Ayuna, Frankie Albert's blood rival for leadership of the mob.

"We believe," Lakis said, "that Richie Miranda, acting on orders, is the one most immediately responsible for the murder of Joe Whitehead and his female companion."

He said Miranda was in custody and being questioned and would likely be charged within twenty-four hours. He added his hope that through plea bargaining Miranda might help him land bigger fish.

Throw in Whitehead's campaign promise to put the screws to the mob, and the result, according to Lakis, was a tidy package that accounted for opportunity and double motive: Ayuna, having got his nephew placed at the Inn through pressure tactics or other means, used him to strike a blow against Albert and rid himself of a threat, in the person of Whitehead, to the mob's enterprises. As for means, the streets of Champaign and Urbana had been awash in Seconal for months; simply everyone had the stuff.

I split when Lakis began taking questions.

In the wake of that press briefing an all but audible sigh of relief rose from the community, one in which I didn't participate. I had heard too much about the connection between Lakis's personal war on the mob and his ambition for higher office to trust his gambit. And the pieces somehow didn't fit together in my mind.

That night, I spotted Harold Bivins passing off duty through the mall, Christmas shopping for all appearances. I joined him in stride and asked for his take on Lakis's theory and how Miranda had responded under questioning.

He stopped. He looked around as if for eavesdroppers and, with lowered voice, told me that Miranda denied everything except being Ayuna's nephew.

"Just between you and me," he said, "I believe the kid, but Lakis is determined to nail him."

Lakis, he said, had picked up on the bit about the door to Whitehead's room not closing all the way; he had hammered Miranda on it in an attempt to get him to confess to waiting until the knockout drops took effect, then coming back and pitching Whitehead off the balcony.

"Miranda held his ground," Bivins said. "He even shot back that he knew damn well some doors in the hotel didn't always close and latch under their own weight. He said some thievery had resulted from that, and he and the other bellhops were under instructions to make sure doors were closed all the way when they left a room, and he was sure he had done so in this case and that the door had to have been unlocked and opened after he made his delivery." Then, as if to go Lakis one better, and in a bold stroke that seemed to have convinced Bivins of his innocence, Miranda told Lakis that any bellhop worth his salt could get into any room any time he wanted.

Bivins said Miranda claimed not to have seen Martha Herrera when he delivered room service, but added that as Whitehead was tipping him he heard the toilet flush behind the closed bathroom door.

As far as Bivins was concerned, Lakis was out there on his own in his attempt to hang the rap on Miranda, playing on the public's concern over the mob and its eagerness to put the matter to rest. And he feared that by sheer force of will, Lakis might pull it off. Bivins winced and bared his teeth, perhaps from the effort required to swallow his principles and let Lakis have his way.

I thought again of that death threat I was carrying around in my sport coat. I didn't relish the thought of sitting on evidence that might prevent Richie Miranda from getting railroaded; neither did I relish the prospect of coming under scrutiny for having withheld it for as long as I had. So I did what any right-thinking citizen would do — I allowed my instinct for self-protection to prevail, rationalizing that what Lakis was about was beyond my control and that if Miranda was innocent he would be cleared, even though I knew the wheels of justice sometimes wobbled.

For a while it worked. I was content to watch with detached curiosity as the case proceeded; amused to see Lakis preen in the spotlight as he rolled forward on the track of his ambitions while pretending to roll back the forces of evil; secure in my distance from the affairs of men, evil, to be sure — content, amused, and secure, that is, until I had an encounter that shook my suspicion that Lakis was wrong and threatened to dislodge me from my detachment.

CHAPTER 15
THE MOBSTER

In the time between the mall's closing and the arrival of the overnight maintenance crew, whoever is working security checks for stragglers and makes sure all the stores are locked and empty.

While engaged in that routine on a night soon after Lakis's press conference, I thought I heard voices come from the rear of Arcadia near the end of the west concourse. The grate was down and locked. I rattled it and yelled back. Jake Duva stuck his head out of his office to say that he was working on books and bundling quarters. That didn't explain why I had heard voices, but I let it go out of deference to Jake, who sometimes let me play for free on Snakepit, a vintage pinball machine at the back of his place.

I eventually worked my way to the corridor behind the row of shops that included Arcadia, to check rear doors. Like others of its kind — narrow and high-ceilinged, painted battleship gray and illuminated by fluorescent lights — that corridor had a surreal, spooky feel to it, and somehow more so at that hour. It would have been an apt setting for a showdown between some poor, average sap and the embodiment of weirdness in a "Twilight Zone" episode. I say this by way of explaining how I felt and reacted when what happened next.

Having just made verbal and visual contact with Jake, it was out of sheer, absent-minded habit that I rattled the knob on Arcadia's back door. It was unlocked. I opened it, remembered Jake, let it close and moved on. Seconds later, it opened behind me. I stopped and turned, expecting Jake, maybe to invite me in for a turn on Snakepit. Instead, the frowning mug that appeared, one I recognized from the pages of the *Chicago Tribune*, belonged to none other than Jimmy "The Lip" Ayuna. He stepped out.

"Help you find something, pal?" he said.

I considered showing my security ID, but Ayuna was rolling the fingers of his right hand, and I thought it best not to go reaching.

"Security," I said. "Just checking to see if everything's locked up." I managed to keep my voice from quaking.

Whatever else I am, I am an American male. I had no sooner spoken than anger rose to my face: I didn't owe a punk thug like Jimmy Ayuna any explanations or apologies for doing my job.

"You got a problem with that?" I heard myself say.

Ayuna stepped toward me, incipient rage on his face.

Jake Duva came out.

"It's okay, Jimmy," he said.

With a look at me that questioned my sanity, Jake led Ayuna back in by the elbow.

I resumed my rounds, shaken but not surprised. As a kid I had known that the pinball games I filled with coins in Newman, as well as the slots in the back room of the American Legion hall and some of the bars — "the machines," as everyone called them — came from Chicago and were owned and managed by the syndicate. How I knew it I can't say; it was simply a given, something everyone knew. So Ayuna's presence at Arcadia seemed as natural as cancer.

Back in my apartment later that night, I remembered seeing the name Ayuna in a headline in the sports section of a recent *News-Gazette*. I dug through a pile on my floor until I found it. The article was a brief piece on Anthony Ayuna, a guard on the Illini's basketball team. He had just been reactivated after recovering from a knee injury. The article mentioned his being from Chicago Heights, where he played at Marian Catholic.

My interest was piqued. From a pay phone carrel in the mall the next evening I called an old college friend who grew up in the Heights and still lived there. He read as many newspapers as I did and had a long and abiding curiosity about the mob, one that derived not so much from civic concern as from a disinterested fascination with criminality and bloody human affairs. I remembered his telling me of the Heights' considerable and ongoing organized crime history: Al Capone had spent some time there; a number of capos live there in harmony with their neighbors, who, like all right-thinking members of the suburban middle class, care only that a homeowner keeps his house and grounds looking tidy and trim. Sure enough, my friend informed me, Anthony Ayuna was Jimmy's son. The Illini played a home game that week, so Ayuna's presence might have been explained on that account.

The next morning, I ran into Harold Bivins at the mall. He said Richie Miranda had made bail. Oh, and by the way, Ken Lakis wanted to interview some people who worked at Lincoln Inn and Lincoln Court, and I was one of them.

Bivins pulled out a notepad; it seemed he was acting as Lakis's appointments secretary. We set up a time on Friday in the Community Room.

My encounter with Jimmy Ayuna had left me wary, and less certain than before that Lakis was sniffing up the wrong tree. Yet now, after seemingly having made up his mind concerning the who, why, and how of Joe Whitehead's murder, he wanted to question people. I couldn't help but wonder if he was hedging his bets against the possibility that his case against Miranda might unravel.

Within me, wariness fought it out with curiosity. Where, I wondered, might I probe with a sharp stick with acceptable risk and reasonable hope of results before my meeting with Lakis?

Of course!

Curiosity won. The question then became, would what killed the cat bring harm to me?

CHAPTER 16
ART

My relationship with Art Ziemann, then in his joyless early sixties and counting the days until retirement, had always been touchy. He frowned at my attire, cringed in puzzlement at my dry, ironic wit (which I could seldom resist employing at his expense), and failed to understand why I couldn't settle down to a sensible career in retail. In uncharitable moments I dismissed him as one of that class of barbarians that doesn't read newspapers.

Not long after talking to Bivins, around noon, I spotted Mindy flouncing out to her car to go to lunch. I decided to pay Art a visit. The outer door was closed but unlocked. I went in. A radio weather report came from the back room. "Anybody home?" I called out as I went back. I leaned in Art's doorway.

Art was working on a sandwich. He swiveled in his chair and looked at me but didn't speak. Uninvited, I sat in the chair on the other side of his desk. He turned off the radio.

I took the sheet with the death threat against Whitehead from the inner breast pocket of my sport coat, unfolded it and held it out for him to take. Art squinted hard at it and wheeled back in his chair. I set the sheet on his desk.

"I guess we don't need this anymore," I said, "now that Lakis has his man. If he does."

He eyed me warily. "What do you mean 'if?"

"Maybe you haven't heard," I said. "Word's going around that you're next on the hit list." His eyes got big; he flared his nostrils and sat up straight. "There's even a sale in the works." I traced a banner in the air. "THE MANAGER'S BEEN SNUFFED — 50% OFF EVERYTHING."

"Don't you have work to do?" Art said. He was perturbed, but also seemed relieved, maybe because he thought I had come in only to needle him.

"Sorry, Art. Bad joke. Believe it or not, I feel for you. Business stinks. Joe Whitehead gets himself murdered on your watch. The mob has been flexing its muscles right here under our noses. Then there's that damn pigeon. It's been flying around loose inside the mall for over a month now. Alice feeds it, and Brazelton's threatening to blow its brains out. I've named it Omega, by the way."

At my mention of the mob Art winced. He leaned toward me over the desk.

"Watch your talk," he said in a fierce whisper.

I looked around for eavesdroppers. "Okay," I whispered back. "Maybe I'm slow, but not until Lakis connected Whitehead's murder to the mob did I put two and two together — Arcadia's sweet lease terms, that labor trouble we had when we resurfaced the parking lots. What are we going to do?"

"We? Do?"

"Sure," I said. "We can't let cheap thugs walk all over decent folks."

Art gripped the edge of his desk so hard that his knuckles turned white.

"Lakis wants me in for questioning tomorrow," I said. "I intend to tell him everything and let him know that he can count on our help."

Art covered his ears and looked as if he might scream.

"This conversation never took place," he said. "I don't know you, and I'm not about to risk a bullet to the brain for your pie-in-the-sky ideas about civic duty. Have your meeting. Be a brave citizen. But you'll be making yourself a target for some very rough boys, and if you so much as mention my name I'll come after you myself." He wagged a finger at the sheet of paper on his desk. "Now get out of here and take that with you."

I assumed the countenance of one chastened yet disappointed and rose from the chair. "Sorry I mentioned it, Art," I said. "Enjoy your lunch."

I picked up the sheet, returned it to the inner pocket of my sport coat, and walked out.

My probe had been based on pure speculation. Art's reaction spoke volumes and suggested that Lakis's theory might not have been made up from whole cloth after all.

CHAPTER 17
CAT AND MOUSE

Out of principle, I showed up ten minutes late to my meeting with Lakis, which was set for nine o'clock on Friday in the Community Room.

Bivins was there too. The three of us sat at one end of a long table. Near me on a small table against a wall was a stack of pamphlets that must have belonged to the Brethren. The cover featured a lurid tableau of suffering souls being herded into the fires of Hell by gleeful, mocking Satan. I hoped it wasn't a foreshadowing of my time on the hot seat with Lakis.

I accepted Bivins's offer of coffee.

"Cream or sugar?"

"Black."

He poured from a stainless-steel carafe into a Styrofoam cup and set it in front of me. When I looked at it, any inclination to cooperate I might have walked in with vanished. My black coffee looked more like weak tea and was clear enough that I could see the bottom of the cup. I made a show of pushing it away.

When the interview commenced, I noted that Bivins had been relegated to the role of recording secretary. It wasn't clear if that represented a promotion or a demotion from appointments secretary.

Lakis began by assuring me that he was certain that Richie Miranda was responsible for the deaths of Joe Whitehead and Martha

Herrera and that Miranda had acted on behalf of his uncle, Jimmy Ayuna. But, he said, he was determined to leave "no stone unturned."

"I want you to think hard," he said with a kind of condescension one might use on a child, in case thinking hard might be beyond my capacity. "Did you see anything around the mall in the time leading up to the murders that struck you as suspicious or out of line? Anything. Especially since Whitehead set up shop here."

Hand to chin, lips pursed, eyes narrowed, I thought hard.

"Now that you mention it," I said, brightening, "for a number of weeks the place had been crawling with Republicans."

Lakis was not amused. Bivins, the tip of his tongue between his teeth, intently recorded my response.

"I understand that the Inn wasn't included in your responsibilities as a security guard," Lakis said. "But did you spend time there in any capacity, official or unofficial?"

I explained that except for rare occasions like the Chamber of Commerce banquet back in October, it was out of my jurisdiction.

" I stop by the Inn desk every day I'm on duty," I said, "to steal newspapers from the complimentary stacks set out for guests. Other than that, I'm seldom over that way."

Lakis sat back and crossed his arms over his chest. Bivins furrowed his brow in puzzlement, as if trying to identify a noise inside his head.

We went around in that vein a while longer, after which Lakis, with undisguised exasperation, made it clear that he had heard enough.

With a sour look, Lakis said that on the chance that I was inclined to be more helpful, I ought to have a phone number I could use to reach him. He took Bivins's notepad, but I held up a hand. I pulled the folded sheet of paper bearing the death threat against Joe

Whitehead from the inside of my sport coat and a pen from my pants pocket and wrote on the back of it as he dictated, then put it back.

I stood. I picked up the cup of what was meant to pass for coffee, used it to water a potted plastic plant near the door, crushed the cup, dropped it in a waste basket, and left.

Out in the hall I spotted Art going into a bathroom.

"Not to worry, Art," I called to him. "I told them everything."

CHAPTER 18
PHANTOM OF THE MALL

Sing, muse, of the cruelty of men and of my suffering at the hands of brainless dolts.

I left the interview with Lakis intending to go upstairs for some time on the terrace to watch for suspicious activity under the guise of drinking coffee, reading newspapers, and shooting the bull with Leo if he was there. After greeting Art I turned a corner in the basement and was literally run into by Steve Childress. He was carrying a lidless paper cup of coffee from Crackers & Crates and was too busy chatting up a comely female colleague of his to watch where he was going.

I went concave, arms spread. Most of the coffee ended up on the front of my white shirt. Luckily for me, it wasn't scalding; unluckily for me, I had little choice but to wear its stain the rest of the day. None, from what I could see, got on Childress. That didn't prevent him from glowering at me as, wordless, he went on. Wordless, I glowered back until he and his partner disappeared into the offices of their firm.

After buttoning my sport coat to hide the stain as best I could, I went into the Squire Shoppe, a haberdashery on the east concourse, hoping to find a shirt on sale to change into. As I reconnoitered, Kurt Scheidler approached.

Scheidler had clerked at the Squire Shoppe through his college days. After graduating he stayed on and worked his way up to assistant manager. He had all the makings of a fine middle-echelon

Nazi, and I sometimes imagined that I'd be punished in the afterlife by having to listen while he prattled on about his superior sartorial taste. There in the pink flesh, he smugged up his face.

"I suppose you and your Democrat friends are happy now that Joe Whitehead's out of the way," he said. "I wouldn't be surprised if it was one of you who killed him."

"You have me wrong, Scheidler," I said. "I've voted straight Rastafarian since '68."

I'd have left things at that, but he looked me up and down with a sneer and said, "You shouldn't even be in here, looking the way you do."

A female customer looked over at us as if our exchange had caught her attention.

"Lady," I said with raised voice, "this man just called you a whore. Say the word and I'll kill him for you."

Her chin dropped. She looked stricken from me to Scheidler and back to me, whether in belief or disbelief I couldn't tell, then fled in tears.

Scheidler flushed all the way up to his scalp. He looked like a scalded albino rat.

I walked out, with no new shirt to change into after all.

About fifteen minutes later, Bill Brazelton was in the Squire Shoppe talking with Scheidler. They stopped talking and watched me as I passed.

I went to the Inn desk to liberate some newspapers and spent the rest of the morning reading and drinking coffee on the terrace, jawing with Leo, and walking rounds. For lunch I ordered takeout from Yen Ching, next to the parking lot on the south side of the mall, and returned to the terrace to eat and read. Brazelton lumbered up, exuding anger and aggression, and stood on the other side of the railing next to my table.

I tried to ignore him by retreating deeper into the newspaper. Boxed in a column under the heading "On This Date in History" were brief descriptions of notable historical events that had taken place on past December ninths. Upon seeing that column, I realized that it was my fortieth birthday. Birthdays, including my own, even the ones with a zero at the end, have never held much significance for me, so the fact registered without resonating.

"I was talking to Scheidler," Brazelton said. "Me and him agree that you ain't as smart you think you are. What I hear is that you never graduated from college, that you was only hanging around to dodge the draft."

"Not true," I said, Ming's Beef dangling from my chopsticks. "I have a B.A. in B.S., an M.A. in Malay, and a PhD. in LSD."

Brazelton wrinkled his nose, furrowed his brow, and squinted, either trying to determine if I were serious or consulting his meager repertoire of ripostes. Finally he huffed, "I bet you don't," and stomped off.

To convey the impact of what happened next, I must first indulge in a bit of confession.

Now, years later, I can see the extent to which, by way of compensation for being an underachiever and a nobody, I had by then assumed a glib, cynical persona and the habit of elevating myself in my own eyes by cutting some poor benighted schmuck off at the knees with the stiletto of my ironic wit. My run-in with Steve Childress aside, how pleased I was with myself to have frustrated Lakis, undone Scheidler, befuddled Brazelton. I daresay I must have smirked inwardly, and maybe outwardly, as I resumed my rounds after eating, my belly full of Chinese food, my fancy full of what a clever fellow I had been.

As I passed Music! Music!, Fran Piper — winsome, risible Fran, with whom I was secretly in love — stood by her register and waved me in. I bade my heart be still and went to her. She drew me close and, in a whisper, told me that a teenage girl at the back of the store had slipped a cassette tape into a pocket of her coat. I hung around close to the front, pretending to shop. The girl came up an aisle and left without going through checkout. As soon as she had both feet on the concourse, I went out, took her by the elbow and told her she'd have to come with me to the mall office.

She tried to pull free. I tightened my grip. She kicked and screamed: "Rape!" Somehow I ended up lifting her from behind in a bear hug. She kicked wildly as I tried to prevent her from breaking my shins.

Brazelton approached from my right. Help at last, I thought. Still holding the girl, I twisted around as best I could to apprise him of the situation, in time to see his meaty fist on its way to my eye. I was out before I hit the concourse.

I awoke under a canopy of faces, one of them Brazelton's with a malevolent grin. He later claimed, with no hint of irony and despite his having seen me only moments before, to have mistaken me for a derelict, what with the day's growth of beard and the stained and rumpled clothes.

Lacking medical benefits, I declined someone's offer to call an ambulance, preferring to take the chance that nothing was broken or concussed. I made my way to the break room, where I spent some time on the couch until my head cleared to the extent that I could almost walk a straight line. I was well short of the end of my shift, but I punched out and caught a bus to Campustown, a trip I always made on foot.

I spent the remainder of that day and evening in my apartment in a futile search for release from pain. Standing, sitting, lying down, my entire head throbbed. I couldn't read. I couldn't think with any sustained clarity. Not until well past midnight was I able to sleep, and then only fitfully, plagued by dreams, among them one involving Beth and Brazelton, who seemed somehow a couple, and one that had me running through dark, unfamiliar streets, shellfire falling all around.

After a few hours I awoke to a knocking sound — from inside my head or outside it, I couldn't tell. I rolled off the side of my futon onto hands and knees and struggled to my feet. I touched my cheekbone below the right eye and gasped. The pain was still intense, but at least more local.

Shivering, I went to the bay window. The time and temperature sign mounted to the bank on a corner across the street showed nineteen degrees. A cold front had moved in. The knocking was my radiator heating up.

I stumbled to the bathroom and stood in front of the mirror. My hair was unruly. The right side of my face was swollen and raw. Phantom of the Mall. I tried brushing my teeth, but every bristle seemed to touch a nerve-end that led straight to the damage on my face. I dampened a washrag and held it there.

Remembering that the day before had been my birthday, I realized that, having attained the age of forty, I had outlived my father. Near what turned out to be the end of his life, with all the wisdom of my fourteen years, I had come to disdain him, to be embarrassed by him, to think of him as a failure. What I saw with brutal, unforgiving clarity that morning was that, in every way that mattered, he was a better man than the one I had become. He had worked hard, supported a family, lived honestly and honorably, been well thought of by his fellow citizens. By contrast, I had grown into a middle adulthood marked by a failed and childless marriage, not one accomplishment to which I could point with satisfaction, a life shored up with rationalizations and sacrificed on the altars of detachment, irony, and cynicism.

I was scheduled to work that morning. I struggled into clothes, made myself as presentable as I could and went downstairs. Outside, I recoiled from the cold and light that on any other day I'd have found bracing. I wasn't up for a repeat of my experience on the bus the day before, when the driver and passengers looked at me and wondered if they should commiserate or keep a safe distance, so I set out on foot.

I trudged down Green Street, my every step pounding in my head. As I passed a pay phone, I considered calling to let Art know I couldn't make it in, but I didn't want to give Brazelton the satisfaction of costing me a full day's pay. A bus stop bench advertisement for Carle Hospital's victim recovery program asked if I were "Abused? Alone?" A poster in a storefront announced a speaker coming to campus to deliver a lecture on "Battered Males — The Invisible Victims." I yearned for invisibility as my battered face looked back at me from window after window.

As I crossed Wright Street, a woman coming the other way gave me a wide berth. At Lincoln Avenue, I came near to being hit by a car coming from my almost blind right side, the blast from its horn reaming the space between my ears.

I stumbled through the mall's west entrance and went to the basement, hoping I'd find the couch in the break room empty so that I could lie down for a few minutes before going on duty. As I passed Art's office, Mindy waved me in.

She looked me up and down with a gossip's curiosity, pursed her lips in satisfaction, and in her grating sing-song delivery said,

"Jerry *Burn*side wants to *see* you."

CHAPTER 19
THE HOT SEAT

Not long after hiring in at Lincoln Court, it became clear that I was acceptable to some of the merchants virtually all of the time, most of the merchants most of the time, and a few squint-minded money-counters none of the time.

Most objectionable to the members of that last group, which included the Squire Shoppe's manager John Day and his minion Kurt Scheidler, was my appearance, specifically my attire. Useless to argue that cotton garments don't need ironing any more than grass needs mowing, one look at me and they counted me a slacker, a hippie, a freethinker, perhaps an anarchist, certainly bad for business.

But I never felt that my position at the mall was tenuous, at least on those grounds. I carried my weight, for one thing. When we had a problem with teenagers hanging out, I was the one who thought of distributing wallet-size code-of-conduct cards and of playing classical music over the public address system. It worked. The teenagers that still came either shopped in earnest or hung out in Arcadia. I also busted my quota of shoplifters, of which we had few. And since my employer, strictly speaking, was Burnside Security and not the mall, and since over the years Jerry Burnside had been satisfied with my work, I enjoyed a kind of qualified immunity. In this case, however, I suspected I'd have to answer for events of the day before.

Jerry's office was in an old brick building on Race Street, near Lincoln Court. I went there prepared for anything but hoping he would accept my side of the story and use it to build a case against Brazelton for the purpose of firing him.

Jerry's secretary gave me a long look. I wanted to attribute it to her shock at the sight of the battered right side of my face, but there was an unsettling something else in it. She let Jerry know by intercom that I had arrived. After making me wait ten minutes, not a good sign, he intercommed back and told her to send me in.

Jerry was at his desk, perusing the contents of an expandable folder. He gestured to the chair across from him. I sat.

"Job applications," he said, shuffling papers. "Qualified people, too. I wish I could hire some of them, but the way things are going I may have to lay off."

Jerry tossed the folder on the desk. He studied my face with as much amusement as commiseration.

"I heard you had a rough time of it yesterday," he said. "That looks nasty."

"Sore as hell," I said. "If you have to lay off, start with Brazelton."

Jerry gave me a non-committal look. He asked me to relate my version of the incident with Brazelton and the girl. I gave it to him straight, trying to keep righteous victimhood out of my voice, adding that I didn't believe for a minute that Brazelton thought I was a derelict.

Jerry acknowledged that I had been in a tough spot and agreed with my assessment of Brazelton's claim.

So far so good, but I sensed that he was only warming up.

"What about before that?" he said.

"Before that?"

He said he had got a call from John Day concerning a woman customer who had been offended by something someone had said in the Squire Shoppe.

"Day was pretty hot," Jerry said. "He got the story from Scheidler, and between the *he saids* and the *she saids* I'm not entirely sure what he thinks happened and who he thinks said what. But he *did* call *me*."

He hadn't asked a question, so I didn't respond.

"Business is bad at the mall," he said.

"I know. It's been that way for a while."

"The merchants are on edge, what with everything else that's been happening."

"Can't blame them. Me too, I guess."

"The axe could fall any day," Jerry said. "No point in making things worse."

"I agree," I said. "Tell you what, I'll try to get to the bottom of what happened at the Squire Shoppe. And if I see the woman who had a bad experience there, I'll even apologize to her, as the mall's representative, so to speak."

"I expect she'd appreciate it," Jerry said. "John Day, too."

"And if I find the wise guy who offended a paying customer, I'll let him know that such conduct is unacceptable."

"Sounds good."

Jerry stood. I stood. We shook hands over his desk. As we did so, I gave Jerry a look intended to convey my commitment to professionalism. However he took it, I interpreted the look he returned, with its one raised eyebrow, to mean that he expected no less.

I had always found Jerry a good guy to work for, always appreciated his maturity, flexibility, and fairness, never more so than on that day. But he was also a businessman with a clientele to answer to.

I left, relieved that the axe that might fall any day wouldn't fall on my neck on that day after all, but very much aware that it was still poised.

CHAPTER 20
SNOOPING

Knowing that I was maybe one screw-up from losing my low-status, minimum-wage job had the effect of concentrating my mind. Especially after my undocking from Beth, that job had served to keep me in shelter, food, and clothing. My disdain for the trappings of the American middle class notwithstanding, I knew I wouldn't take well to sleeping outdoors in cardboard boxes and rummaging in dumpsters for meals. Yet with no college degree and virtually no marketable skills to speak of, I couldn't help but imagine someday having to make my way in the world in such a manner if I got canned. Of course if Lincoln Court went belly up, as seemed likely, I'd be out of a job anyway. But better to lose it to something I couldn't control than to something I could but failed to.

Not that I left Jerry's office intent on redeeming myself by trying to solve what I still considered to be unsolved murders. Far from it. With all that had happened in the past twenty-four hours, I had more or less forgotten about the case.

But when I got to work, there was Bivins as I had seen him in recent days, trailing Lakis through the mall like an obedient puppy, listening and nodding and taking notes as Lakis spoke. From all appearances, he had either got over his misgivings about Lakis's targeting of Miranda or repressed them. And he hadn't followed up on his request that I keep my eyes and ears open and report to him anything I might think pertinent to the case.

In fact, I had absorbed a considerable amount of scuttlebutt without even trying. In the time since the deaths of Joe Whitehead and Martha Herrera, the mall had been rife with rumor and speculation regarding every aspect of the case: the guilty party, apparent motives, hidden motives, plots and conspiracies of every kind. Seemingly everyone had a theory — the very walls seemed to give them off — and the urge to declaim it.

Most people, though, fell into one of two camps, those who bought into Lakis's charge against Miranda and the mob and those convinced that Roger Worthington had either done the job or hired someone to do it for him.

Yet neither of those lines of thinking sounded convincing to me. In my estimation, Lakis erred in believing, or pretending to believe, that the most important question was, Who had a motive for killing Joe Whitehead and Martha Herrera? and that the answer to that question was the mob. I had a strong hunch that Martha Herrera had been an innocent victim, in the wrong place at the wrong time. I was sure, too, that the mob guys, myopic though they were, could see Whitehead's railing against them as so much campaign rhetoric and not a real threat. Indeed, he hadn't spoken a word on the subject since the election. Besides, slipping him a Mickey and pitching him off the balcony of his room wasn't their style; they usually preferred the quick efficiency of a bullet to the brain.

Adding spice to the mix was Mary Cobb's theory that Whitehead had been a victim of his inability to keep his penis in his pants. "One even hears," she informed me one day — I hadn't asked — savoring the morsel before rolling it off her tongue, "that Joe Whitehead was doing to Steve Childress what Steve Childress did to you." She watched to see if I would squirm at the reminder.

Yes, one did hear that. One had *been* hearing that since summer. For that matter, if the rumors of Beth's sexual involvement with both Whitehead and Worthington were true — or even if they weren't true, as long someone believed them — not only did Worthington have one more motive, but the list of suspects grew: Steve Childress, the jealous husband; Suzy Whitehead, the betrayed wife; who knew, maybe even Beth, who might fear that public knowledge of an affair with Whitehead would trip her up on her way to the top of whatever ladder she was climbing.

When it came to motive, the likeliest was Worthington, yet I was convinced he had neither done the deed nor had it done, despite his beef with Whitehead and despite what I had heard by eavesdropping and other means. He might have been pleased to see Whitehead get his, but if compelled to do something about it himself, he'd likelier have knocked him out with a right hook of the kind I had seen him use on one of his foremen years before. Steve Childress lacked the brains to execute the act on the one hand or the guts to put his pretty self at risk on the other. Clearly, Suzy Whitehead lacked the brains.

I dismissed what the cops were saying as political expediency and most of what I was hearing around the mall as the idle speculation of busybodies. Yet all that speculation and talk, especially when combined with the little secret I still carried in the breast pocket of my sport coat, managed somehow to work its way into my thinking and form rings around a bull's eye that hadn't yet come into focus — a hunch wrapped in a guess inside a feeling, an itch I couldn't quite locate to scratch.

Thomas Merton tells of the time when, in a quandary over whether he was called to a life of silence, he opened his Bible at random and, with eyes shut, put his finger down on the verse, "Behold, thou shalt be silent." Feeling ripe for something equally as serendipitous to cut through the thicket, I turned a corner and came upon Alice on a bench.

Turbaned and layered with mismatched clothes, her shopping bag at her feet, she mumbled to herself as she applied lipstick to her fallen face without the aid of a compact mirror. I stood nearby, outside her range of vision. Who knew but what, much madness being divinest sense, her babble might prove oracular.

I had to listen well, for on that day she spoke more under her breath than in her usual urgent, paranoid squawk. From what I could gather, her gibberish consisted of a complaint over stomach pain, a lament for a late husband, and something dire concerning either *the* sun or *a* son. From her bag she produced the remainder of a roll of toilet paper, unwrapped some sheets around two bony fingers, and dabbed excess lipstick from her mouth. She rose, lifted her bag and shuffled off. Oracular or not, her message was beyond my powers to decode.

Later that day, Leo and I were reading newspapers and drinking coffee on the terrace. In the *News-Gazette*'s sports section, a display ad for the Downtowner Escort Service caught my eye.

"Does it strike you as peculiar," I said to Leo, "that the Downtowner is open for business in spite of being implicated in a murder investigation?"

Leo put his *Trib* down and gave me a knowing smile. "Not if what they say about the Champaign cops is true, it doesn't."

"What is it they say?"

"That the cops wink at what goes on at the Downtowner for a piece of the action, in both senses of the term. Why do you think they took that gal that was found up in Whitehead's room to a hospital in Champaign?"

"You'll have to tell me."

"So Champaign cops could stand guard over her and keep her story from coming out. You ain't heard that?"

I hadn't. Curious and interesting indeed, and, for lack of anything better to go on, a place to start.

CHAPTER 21
STAKEOUT

The Downtowner occupied a storefront two blocks north of Champaign's central business district. Across from it, wedged between two streets that converged at a sharp angle, was a small city park with a bench and a picnic table under some trees. On a cloudy, cold weekday morning off from work, I filled my Thermos and bought a *Chicago Tribune* at a drug store down on the street and set out on foot in watch cap and pea coat. I got there a little after nine and sat at the picnic table, facing The Downtowner.

The park was empty except for me. Pedestrian traffic was light, as was traffic on the streets. A police squad car slowed as it passed. The cop in the passenger seat gave me a long look.

At ten o'clock, a car pulled up and parked in front of The Downtowner. A tall blond female got out and let herself in with a key. She raised the blind in the front window, turned on the lights, and took off her overcoat. With the newspaper spread out before me to make it look like I was reading, I watched as she made coffee and worked at a desk.

The cops who had cruised by and given me the eye came by again and stopped. They got out and walked over.

"Good morning," the taller one said. "Can I see your driver's license?"

"I don't have one," I said. I took my wallet from my back pocket, took out my library card and handed it to him. "I hope this will do."

He looked at it and showed it to the other. The second cop spoke: "Can you tell us what you're up to here, Mr. Cleary?"

Their manner wasn't overbearing, but I didn't much appreciate having my right to be there challenged. Then it occurred to me that they might be cozy with The Downtowner, and I checked my impulse to mouth off.

"I'm drinking coffee and reading the newspaper."

The tall cop spoke again: "We have some questions we'd like to ask you. The best place to do that is at the station. It's close by. When we're done, we can bring you back here. If you don't mind."

"Do I have a choice?"

The tall one smiled.

At the station I was taken to an interrogation room and told to sit tight. After about ten minutes a cop I hadn't seen yet came in and sat across from me. He looked like Joseph Goebbels, with sunken cheeks, dark, oily hair and the haunted eyes of someone fearful that people were talking about him behind his back. Our dislike for each other was immediate, visceral, and strong.

He told me in an accusatory tone that a mugging and robbery had taken place in that park a few nights earlier and that I fit the description of the perpetrator. I had been working at the time in question and suggested he call Art at the mall to confirm my alibi. He said he'd think about it. In the meantime, he thought I might benefit from some time in a cell with "Pancho Villa." As he escorted me he made a passing remark to another cop about "letting Victor have some company."

He put me in a cell with a young, slender, dark-skinned guy in tight jeans and a polyester shirt, open at the chest. He had black hair slicked back and a thin mustache and was smoking a cigarillo.

"Are you Victor Herrera?" I said.

"I am he," he said, lifting his chin and blowing smoke from one side of his mouth. He smoked like someone who had practiced in front of a mirror.

"I'm with security at Lincoln Court," I said. "I was on the scene when your sister was found unconscious." I lowered my voice to sympathetic-confidential. "A terrible thing. I'm trying to find out who killed her and why."

I hoped he might have something for me, no matter how slight. Victor, however, seemed less interested in learning who was responsible for the death of his sister than in plotting "venganza" against the cop who had called her a whore. I got the impression that the cause of defending his sister's honor was a pretext for Victor to display intensity and passion and pride, that without such a pretext he'd be intense and passionate and proud about nothing in particular. I liked him, though. He made smoking look terrific.

After almost half an hour in the cell, I was released. One of the cops had called Art. Somewhat to my surprise, he had backed me.

On my way out, Joe Goebbels snarled a warning that he'd be watching me. No one offered me a ride back to the park. My enthusiasm for staking out The Downtowner was gone anyway, so I walked home.

That was okay. I think well when I walk. Among the things I thought on my way back to Urbana was that I wanted a closer look at The Downtowner, maybe in the form of time with someone on the inside. Martha Herrera's death had almost certainly had a chilling effect on her colleagues, so I wasn't hopeful that any one of them would be willing to discuss it. Then again, I might get lucky. One thing was certain — I'd never find out if I didn't try.

CHAPTER 22
THE DOWNTOWNER
ESCORT SERVICE

My look at The Downtowner's operation had been brief and through a window from across the street, so I didn't know what to expect when I walked in a couple of days later. Certainly not a bordello parlor with someone knocking out honky-tonk at an upright piano and drunken businessmen slurring love talk to naughty ladies in satin and lace. But neither was I prepared for what I found: modern furniture, artsy prints in stylish frames on the walls, *Forbes* and *Barron*'s in plastic binders.

The blond I had seen the day before was on the phone. The nameplate on her desk bore the name Kristen. She put her hand over the speaker and mouthed to me, "I'll be right with you."

I sat and picked up a copy of *Vanity Fair* and thumbed through it until she hung up. She stood and smiled, successfully disguising whatever effort it took not to notice my bruised and lacerated face.

"Welcome to The Downtowner," she said. "How can we be of help?"

She was taller than me and dressed in all black. Her makeup and hair, pulled back tight, seemed designed to enhance her severity more than any beauty she might be said to have. On my way there I had considered trying the direct approach by asking whoever I met to comment on Lakis's claim that the Downtowner was a mob front for prostitution. But Kristen looked like she was capable of chewing me up and spitting me out, so I played the role of customer.

"This may sound odd," I said, "but I'm looking for someone, a lady, to talk with over coffee."

"That doesn't sound odd at all," she said. She sat and set her fingers above the keyboard. "May I have your name?"

I gave it to her.

She talked as she typed.

"You should know, Mr. Cleary, that we have a minimum four-hour contract. You're free to spend less time of course, or more, but we must charge for at least four hours."

"No problem," I said. "At how much per hour?"

"Hourly rates start at seventy-five dollars. For special events that might require extra preparation or evening attire, it's somewhat more, but it sounds like what you have in mind would qualify for the minimum."

"That's good," I said. "Casual would be appropriate for the place I have in mind. Jeans, even."

She opened a side drawer of her desk, pulled out an album bound in Leatherette and handed it to me.

"If you'd like, you can view in private in that room over there. Turn on the light as you go in."

The room was like an enclosed library carrel, with a windowless door, a padded folding chair and a desk. I sat and opened the album. Inside were photographs in plastic covers, each with a first name and a brief biographical sketch. I leafed through them looking for something that suggested accessibility, sensitivity, openness — somebody who looked like she might be receptive to my inquiry. There were about three dozen pictures in all — no last names, no ages; some full-body shots, some only shoulders up. A few affected come-hither looks. All of them, I suppose, would have been attractive to someone.

Among those who looked like they might meet my criteria was a redhead, in soft focus, hugging a tree: "Jenny's a nature-lover. She likes to ride horses, hike, and swim." Then a blond with short hair and tortoise-shell glasses, posed hand to chin in close-up: "Terri loves good books, but even more, good conversation." A black woman with high cheek bones and penetrating eyes: "With a master's degree in psychology, LaTasha loves spectator sports — when she's not competing herself."

About two thirds of the way through, I found her.

"Emily," the blurb read, "is a law student with an interest in helping the disadvantaged." She had dark hair, cut close and short. No sepia or soft focus for her, rather a clear-eyed, no-nonsense look that conveyed intellect and sexuality. I thought of all the ways I was disadvantaged.

I went out and returned the album to Kristen.

"Who would you like to have coffee with, Mr. Cleary?"

"Tell me about Emily."

Kristen gave me a knowing smile. "Emily is one of our more popular girls," she said. "What evening did you have in mind?"

"What evening is she available?"

CHAPTER 23
ALL I WANTED

There I was, forty going on fourteen, preparing for my first night out with a woman in more than ten years. Light can be manipulated, prints doctored. If no such tricks had been used on Emily's album picture I'd be having coffee with a first-rate beauty.

Twice at the mall I picked up a phone to call and cancel; both times I hung up without making the call. In my apartment on the night in question I paced and fidgeted, rehearsed dialogue, worked like a sculptor at getting my hair right.

Per arrangement, I arrived in a cab at The Downtowner. Through the window in the front door, I could see Emily waiting inside. As I exited the cab, she came out. We met halfway up the sidewalk, shook hands, and introduced ourselves. It was dark, but nearby streetlights allowed me to see that she was about five-two, doe-eyed, and with delicate facial bone structure. The intellect and sexuality I saw in the photo translated well to the live person. I couldn't resist stealing sidelong glances at her in the back seat of the cab as we rode to Campustown.

We got out in front of Coffee Cat on Green Street, which I had chosen for being familiar, comfortable territory. It was frequented mostly by students who, as with my generation, fancy that they have invented rebelliousness, but the coffee is powerful stuff, the ambience artfully subdued, the music by Miles, Monk, Bird. We went in and found a table. She took off her coat. She was slender and shapely in charcoal linen pants and a green silk top.

Emily proved adept at conversation, and her manner betrayed no hint of her being on assignment or of my being a client. With a sympathetic look, she touched the spot on her face equivalent to where mine was bruised and expressed her hope that I hadn't been fighting.

"I didn't get a chance to," I said, and left it at that.

A waiter appeared. I ordered house blend, she decaffeinated French roast. We studied the menu and, when the coffee came, ordered cherry cheesecake and a chocolate torte, under the agreement that we'd split both.

We spent the next fifteen minutes dividing the treats and talking of superficial matters. By the time our cups were refilled, we had established what felt to me like an amiable rapport, so much so that I had almost forgot that she might be a prostitute and that the evening was costing me more than three-hundred dollars.

Before I could find a way to broach the subject of her employer and her dead former colleague, she put me even further at ease.

"This is nice," she said with an appreciative look around. "An informal night out with good coffee and conversation."

She seemed entirely earnest and sincere, more so than I'd have expected from a paid escort. Then it occurred to me that part of her job was to contribute to a relaxed atmosphere and the comfort of her client and that she had done exactly that. Perhaps I was being cynical, but the effect of that thought process was to cool my ardor and help me focus on the task at hand. I thought I saw a way from her remark to my agenda.

"Maybe I'm out of line in saying this," I said, "but you must have to put up with a lot, in your job, I mean."

She rolled her beautiful eyes and shook her head half an inch to each side.

"You wouldn't believe," she said. "Or maybe you would. The hardest to take are the business types."

"Hard in what way?" I said.

"The usual ego stuff." She dropped her voice. "'You're lucky to be out with me, baby. I'm going places.' That or they want to talk about their awful jobs or wives and complain that nobody understands them. And usually over alcohol, which makes things worse." She wrinkled her fine nose. "I probably shouldn't be talking like this. All I'm saying is, this is a nice departure from that scene."

"If you don't mind my asking," I said, "why do you put up with it? I might be assuming too much, but something tells me you have choices."

I expected to have overstepped my bounds, for her to finesse the question or change the subject, but she didn't. She sipped coffee and looked at me straight on.

"Law school's expensive," she said. "I've always got my eye out. Modeling is a possibility, but this isn't exactly New York. At least for now it's a living, a decent enough one that I'm willing to take the bad with the good."

"And hope that what happened to Martha Herrera won't happen to you?"

She was suddenly serious.

"That's an unpleasant subject," she said, not unpleasantly. "You'll understand if I avoid it."

"Sorry," I said. "I hope I haven't spoiled things."

We drank coffee through a moderately awkward silence, which she finally broke.

"Look, I'm sorry too. It's just that what happened to Martha Herrera is a sort of remote occupational hazard, and not exactly a pleasant subject for conversation."

"I'll level with you," I said. "For my own reasons, which I don't expect you to find interesting, I'm trying to learn who killed Martha Herrera and why."

"I thought the killer was in custody."

"Don't believe it."

"Are you a cop or something?"

"Or something. Can we talk?"

"We can talk around it," she said, "but I'm not in a position to tell you much, and I probably wouldn't even if I were. I don't have a reason not to believe you, but I'm not going to compromise myself."

"I won't ask you to."

The waiter came and refilled our cups.

"How long had Martha Herrera been with The Downtowner?" I said. "As far as you knew, was she in good graces with your employer? Did any of the others talk about her and Whitehead?"

"I'm afraid I can't help you, even if I wanted to. I honestly don't know the answers to those questions. Kristen pretty much runs things, and almost never are two of us there at the same time. I think they're concerned that we're going to form a union or something."

"Who are they? Who do you work for?"

"I work for The Downtowner Escort Service."

She sounded like a soldier giving name, rank, and serial number.

"I know that, but who pulls the strings? If Kristen runs things in the office, who runs Kristen? Who signs the paychecks?"

She smiled and shook her head.

"Sorry, you've hit the wall. I don't know what goes on above me and I don't ask. I have a job to do and I do it. I think I do it well and that my employer thinks so too. That's all I know and all I care to know."

"And all it's safe to know?"

"What do you mean?"

"If the cops are right, above you are some rough boys, and by working for them you're involved in what they're involved in, whether you like it or not."

She was unfazed.

"My size notwithstanding," she said, "I'm pretty good at taking care of myself. What if I told you that if you're right, those rough boys wouldn't appreciate your snooping into their business?"

"I'd believe you."

I dropped the subject. I hadn't learned all I wanted to, but, clearly, all I was going to. I knocked back the last of my coffee.

"Let's take a walk," I said.

She brightened as fast as she had earlier grown serious. I paid and we left. Almost three hours remained on my time.

The sidewalks were filled with students. Emily took my arm and gave it a squeeze.

"I'm sorry I couldn't be of more help," she said. "What I said earlier still stands. This is my idea of a nice evening. I hope it's not over."

I started to say something, but it didn't get past my throat. I felt like Tony in West Side Story when he sees Maria at the dance — people all around but eyes for only her.

"We have some time left," she said. "Was that all you wanted, just to talk?"

I stopped. I checked my watch, took a slow, deep breath, looked up and down the street, examined my shoes, all in an effort to compose an answer that came from above the belt.

I have never understood the attraction by men to prostitutes who slather themselves with makeup, poof their hair, wobble around on stiletto heels in skin-tight synthetics. Such was not Emily, if prostitute she was, so fetching there before me with her coat open over simple, tasteful linen and silk.

Was that all I wanted?

We were near the door that led up to my apartment, which she would have no way of knowing. Or would she? Maybe The Downtowner had compiled a dossier on me that included my address and how horny I was likely to be. It occurred to me that I might subconsciously have chosen Coffee Cat for its proximity to my place.

Was that all I wanted?

As of that question I had not enjoyed the intimate company of a woman in a very long time. Not that I went about with a permanent erection, but at times, and never more so than with Emily, I felt like I had semen backed up to my brain.

Was that all I wanted?

A cab approached. I waved it over. It stopped. I stepped to the curb and opened the door and gestured for Emily to enter.

She got in. I handed the cabby a ten-dollar bill and said to him, "She'll tell you where." Emily looked coolly straight ahead. I shut the door. The cab drove off. I stuffed my hands into my pants pockets and walked down the street among the students.

I considered going back into Coffee Cat or up to my apartment, but opted instead to stay out in the mid-December air a while longer, hoping it might have the same effect as a cold shower.

CHAPTER 24
IN STITCHES

In spite of my working part time at a minimum-wage job, I saw fit to spend more than three-hundred dollars on a night out with a paid escort because the rent for my Campustown apartment was low, I didn't own a car, and I contributed little to the retail and service economies. As a result, in the years since becoming single again I have saved much more money than I have spent.

My first move after being discarded by Beth was into the YMCA. I took with me not much more than the clothes I wore and what I could stuff into a duffel bag. I had been there a short while when one day, while browsing in Wordsworth and Company bookstore on Green Street, I overheard Tom Franklin, the owner of the building, speaking to a store clerk about the unused space three floors above. I asked him about it, explaining that I was looking for a place to live and that that area would suit me well. He took me up to check it out.

It amounted to a single large room with a bay window overlooking the street. It was dusty and cluttered with empty cardboard boxes and some other junk. Tom assured me that beneath the mess it was in good shape. He said that for him it was wasted space and that he'd convert the plumbing to residential use, partition off a bathroom, and give me a break on the rent if I would pitch in on cleaning the place up and agree to a long-term lease. He suggested three years. I suggested five. We shook hands. I signed papers the next day. Within a week I was moved in.

And here I am still, four floors above Green Street in the heart of Campustown. The bookstore is still at street level, but a variety of tenants have come and gone from the other two floors. Currently, Julia's Closet, a vintage clothing and consignment shop, occupies the second floor. Between it and me Ramona gives massages and practices personal growth counseling through hypnosis and dream and aroma therapy.

Except for a desk and a padded armchair, a small table with a lamp, the futon on which I sleep, and a mini-fridge, I have kept my place in an unfurnished simplicity that I've come to think of as Zen-Shaker. The floors are bare planks; the walls and ceiling, which I painted, are off white (Bone White, to be precise, #YF20 from the True Value Hardware store down the street) and free of adornment. In the center of the high ceiling is an incandescent light bulb covered with a milky globe, on the inside bottom of which rest the carcasses of numerous insects. I have a small radio, but no stereo, telephone, television or major appliances. A built-in linen closet holds the few clothes I own and some towels and washcloths. I like knowing that if I needed to I could be ready in little more time than it will have taken to write this paragraph to move across town or across the country.

In my years here I have spent countless waking hours in my bay window, reading, scribbling, listening to classical music and jazz on the radio, and watching in wonder and amusement at life down on the street. I have witnessed fistfights, a stabbing, a couple of shootings, a near rape in the back seat of a car in full daylight, armed robbery, vehicular and mob violence, but mostly the everyday human traffic one might expect to find in a commercial district adjacent to a university campus of more than 40,000 students.

Sartre, I believe it is, has something to say about the salutary effect of elevated perspectives that may have bearing here. Whatever the reason, I have found the entire spectacle consistently diverting and amusing.

Students from a variety of tribes — scholars, preppies, jocks, Bohemians — strut and pose, and I laugh until my face is wet with tears. Bankers and lawyers, including Beth and Steve, march in purposeful strides to and from lunch, and it's all I can do to keep from rolling on the floor.

I once heard a preacher who claimed to be engaged in daily conversation with God speak of the tears God sheds over how far His creation has fallen. I buy the part about the tears, but I've come to suspect it's likelier that God is in stitches.

In relating all this, I don't mean to sound arch or detached or philosophical; I'm not the least inclined to philosophy, despite having majored in the subject for a time. And if I come off as self-absorbed or odd or even lunatic, so it goes. I have long since relinquished hope of making rational connection to my fellow rational creatures.

At any rate, I have come to consider the time I spend in my bay window as a kind of vocation, and I am deeply grateful to Beth and Steve for their part in helping me find it. If I never told them so, it was not out of bitterness. It's just that they always had so much on their minds, were wary enough of me already, and I didn't wish to confuse them.

CHAPTER 25
VICIOUS, VINDICTIVE, MEAN-SPIRITED, LOW

In the insular world of Lincoln Court, Joe Whitehead's demise was reduced to fuel for rumor, gossip, innuendo, and vulgar speculation. In Springfield, however, Republicans and Democrats insisted on treating it as a consequential matter and were busy going at each other's throats over who would succeed to the governorship, and when and how.

Article V, Section 6(a), of the Illinois Constitution has this to say about gubernatorial succession: "In the event of a vacancy, the order of succession to the office of Governor or to the position of Acting Governor shall be the Lieutenant Governor." Citing that wording, the Republicans asserted that on inauguration day Lieutenant Governor-elect Wilson Manning should be sworn in to the office to which he was elected, then, the governorship being vacant, sworn in as governor.

The Democrats disagreed. The clear intention of the Constitution, they said, was for the lieutenant governor to succeed a sitting governor; they noted the custom of the governor's being sworn in before the lieutenant governor and argued that the reverse was logically insupportable: Without a governor to swear in, there could not, strictly speaking, be a lieutenant governor, and thus no succession could take place.

Citing Article V, Section 2, of the Illinois Constitution, which states that "...elected officers of the Executive Branch shall hold office for four years... until their successors are qualified," the Democrats put forward a plan they billed as a noble compromise and, given their distaste for the incumbent administration, no small sacrifice on their part: There being no qualified successor, Republican Governor George Foley should retain office until a special election could be held. They submitted the proposal to the Illinois Election Board for a ruling. Its response, amounting to entire befuddlement, was to issue as many opinions on the legality, necessity, and timing of such an election as there were board members.

The Republicans accused the Democrats of cynicism, calling their plan a thinly disguised attempt at getting another shot at putting one of their own in the governor's mansion. They countered that Whitehead's death before taking office was a mere technicality, that had he died the day after the inauguration, or the hour after, the lieutenant governor would have succeeded him.

The Republican-controlled state Senate sponsored a resolution stating that the will of the people would be usurped if the lieutenant governor-elect were not allowed to assume the governorship. It passed along strict party lines. The House, controlled by the Democrats, sponsored a resolution stating that the will of the people would be usurped if he were. It too passed along strict party lines, but not before fisticuffs erupted on the House floor.

In all, the affair was exemplary of Illinois politics at its most entertaining — vicious, vindictive, mean-spirited, and low.

The issue was finally resolved when the Illinois Supreme Court granted a hearing in a suit brought by the League of Women Voters for the purpose of settling the matter for the public good. In a five-to-two opinion, the Court ruled that the Republican view prevailed. Wilson Manning was to be sworn in as lieutenant governor, then immediately sworn in as governor. The then-vacant lieutenant governor's office would remain so for the remainder of the term, consistent with Article V, Section 7, of the Illinois Constitution.

Among the busybodies and gossips at Lincoln Court, Wilson Manning, whose long-standing ambition for the governorship was well known, became for a while the latest suspect in the murder of Joe Whitehead.

CHAPTER 26
MICHAEL PARISH

For a number of days, Ken Lakis had been publicly silent about the murders. Some of the speculation at the mall suggested that his theory about Richie Miranda and the mob connection had proven to have too many holes in it but that Lakis was too proud and embarrassed to admit it. My own investigation, such as it was, had gone nowhere, and I had all but given it up.

Such was the state of affairs when I joined Leo on the terrace about a week before Christmas.

With a pull of his head, he directed my attention to a nearby table, where Karl Thomaczec sat with another old retiree. Karl was in a lather. I heard him spit the word *Jap*.

"If you don't want another murder on your hands," Leo said, "you might have to put the arm on Karl."

Gaunt and hobbled, Karl was a bitter, angry old cuss who had never forgiven the Japanese for the rough time they gave him in a POW camp during World War II.

"The slant-eyed son-of-a-bitch gets too close to me," Karl said, "I'll send him home in a box."

I shot a questioning look at Leo. He folded open the business section of his *News-Gazette* to an inside page and handed it over to me with his finger on a story.

Citing Roger Worthington as its source, it told of the coming of Satoshi Matsuta, a representative of the Kitsu Corporation of Japan, to determine the extent of his employer's possible investment in Worthington's Lincoln Center project. Kitsu, according to the piece, was a world leader in electronics and aerospace technology that had recently been acquiring American real estate, including Parish National Golf Course, and was negotiating with the Parish family for stakes in more of its holdings.

I recalled what Beth had said the night I broke into Worthington's office about Charlotte Parish and her brother being "ready to deal" and the coming of someone named Matsuta to "look the place over."

Later I went to the Inn desk for a *Chicago Tribune*. While I was there, a man appeared on my right and told Felix, the desk clerk, that he had a reservation. He was tall, well fed and well heeled, and on the far side of middle age, with thin reddish hair going to gray. He looked vaguely familiar, but I couldn't conjure a name. As Felix got him registered, I went to a chair and sat. I opened the *Trib*, more to eavesdrop from behind it than to read. I heard the jangle of a key on a holder.

"Your room is ready, Mr. Parish," Felix said. "Do let us know if you need anything."

Felix hit the bell. A bellhop appeared and took the guest's luggage. They got on an elevator.

I went to the desk. "Who was that?" I asked Felix.

Felix raised his eyebrows. "*That's* Michael Parish," he said.

My eyebrows went up. *The* Michael Parish? The moneyed leftist and scourge of the American political right wing? The Michael Parish with Hanoi and Havana stickers on his luggage, who marched arm in arm with Jerry Rubin and the yippies in Chicago in 1968? Who renounced and denounced his capitalist legacy to the great shame of his capitalist family and used his considerable inheritance to fund radical causes?

Some weeks earlier I had read a newspaper review of a recent book by Michael Parish, *What's Left?*, a manifesto for America's radical left wing in the wake of the Reagan Revolution. It would be intriguing indeed if the author of that book and the Michael Parish who had just then checked into the hotel were the same person, even more intriguing if he were connected to the Parish family that owned Lincoln Inn and Lincoln Court. The review had contained passing reference to a feature on Michael Parish in a recent issue of *Vanity Fair*.

The next morning, on my way to work, I stopped at the Urbana public library and looked up the *Vanity Fair* piece. It was a combined retrospective, psychobiography, and update on Michael Parish's career as a radical activist, with family history sketched into the background.

Michael Parish was born into serious money in 1922, the second child of his father Edmund's second wife, the first child being his sister Felicity. His father's first wife, a manic depressive, had borne a pair of her own, Charlotte and Nolan, before committing suicide.

Felicity and Michael grew to be twins in spirit and temperament and, increasingly, apart from and at odds with Nolan and Charlotte. As long as their differences were over dolls and toy trucks, no great harm was done. By the time they had all reached adulthood, which is not to say maturity, the animosity between them was deep and bitter, only now with the family fortune at stake.

Michael went to Harvard but left and joined the army when America entered World War II, itching to have a go at the Japanese for their role in the undoing of his sister Felicity, whose acting career and happy life, according to the article, came crashing down around her at Pearl Harbor on December 7, 1941. He was sent to Europe instead and was part of an Allied group that liberated some Nazi death camps in the waning days of the war, an experience that may have come close to unhinging his already delicate psyche.

Edmund Parish retired from active involvement in business affairs after the end of the war. Concerned that the malice between his sets of children might lead to ruin, he declined to transfer his holdings, consisting mainly of commercial real estate, all of a piece to them as joint heirs. Rather, with two exceptions, he divided and dropped them on both sides of the battle line. Nolan and Charlotte got two thirds in common, Michael the remaining third. (Felicity's mental impairment was such that she received nothing in her own name, but her welfare was seen to.)

The more notable of the two exceptions was Parish National Golf Course near Naperville. Its great worth was such that an even split would have been impossible, so it was left in common to Charlotte, Nolan, and Michael in the hope that they would rise above their differences and maintain it with dignity.

The other exception, described as "some property in Downstate Illinois," seemed to have been set aside for the welfare of Felicity, who was believed to be living in seclusion there under the care of family staff. Nolan, Charlotte, and Michael were enjoined to administer it in her best interests. An anonymous source close to the family speculated that this arrangement was Edmund Parish's last hope for fostering a bond between his offspring.

In the fifteen years after Michael Parish received his $140 million inheritance — the third that wasn't in joint ownership — he suffered depression, philandered his way through multiple wives and mistresses, consumed barrels of booze, dabbled in communal living, esoteric religions, and radical politics, all the while delegating business matters in which he had no interest to men in gray suits with whom he had no affinity.

Not long after his mother and father died in 1959 in a boating accident, Michael sold off his inheritance to parties outside the family in order to shed what he called "the mantle of capitalist exploiter," leaving Nolan and Charlotte to lament that he had allowed Parish property to pass into "unworthy hands." At the same time, he signed over to them his share of Parish National Golf Course, "that gross symbol of capitalism," declining compensation as a show of disdain. Now in his forties, the century's Sixties, he entered analysis, emerging after eighteen months an ultra-liberal political activist.

From his estate in Bel Aire, he used some of his cash to found his own publishing house and film production company. He specialized in documentary films and books, some of which he authored himself, which exposed what he believed to be the evils of capitalism. He showed up in Havana in the mid-1960s, later in Hanoi. (Strawberry-haired and left-handed, his conservative detractors referred to him alternately as Red and Lefty.) His ventures lost money, but at such a rate that it wasn't likely to run out before he did.

An unnamed family friend who maintained ties on both sides accused him of hypocrisy, citing his multiple cars and houses and his private jet.

"For all his contempt for Nolan and Charlotte," the friend was quoted as saying, "Michael's a lot like them. He comes off as salt of the earth, but one glimpse of how he treats the hired help and you can see that he assumes others were born to serve him. I think he salves his conscience with his politics."

Over the years, fueled by spite, the half-siblings found numerous reasons to sue each other, resulting in the transfer of a significant chunk of their respective fortunes to lawyers. Perhaps for that reason, Nolan and Charlotte sold Parish National to Links International, headquartered in Tokyo, for around $500 million.

Now it was Michael's turn to bemoan the hands into which Parish property had fallen.

Links International was a subsidiary of Kitsu, a Japanese conglomerate. Until the 1950s, when it began to diversify and expand overseas, Kitsu had been primarily a manufacturing concern. In the 1930s it had made parts for Mitsubishi's Zero, one of the planes used in the attack on Pearl Harbor. Michael lamented that had he known that Nolan and Charlotte were capable of being so insensitive to Felicity he'd never have given up his one-third share in Parish National. He expressed concern that they might even be capable of selling off their two-thirds stake in "the Urbana property, Felicity's last refuge," leaving him, and her, at the mercy of whoever would then have majority control.

The article ended with mention of Michael Parish's then-forthcoming book, *What's Left?*, which signaled his emergence from a reclusive decade with a fresh commitment to his leftist political ideology.

I closed the magazine. In a few minutes I had to be at work at the mall. For me at least, the place would be charged with the intriguing likelihood that the Michael Parish I had just read about was in town and staying at Lincoln Inn. Clearly, he was not only *not* the brother that was "ready to deal" that Beth had referred to, but had strong reasons to oppose any such deal. And it appeared that his presence there would coincide with the coming of a representative of the Kitsu Corporation for the purpose of negotiating that deal.

Some popular somebody I had never heard of stared up from the magazine cover with exaggerated, ironic inquisitiveness. He might have been asking my question: What in *hell* is Michael Parish doing in Urbana? I left the library with the foreboding that the answer to that question might be written in blood.

CHAPTER 27
MOTHER-DAUGHTER DAY

All that day I kept an eye out for Michael Parish and for Japanese men but spotted neither. I spotted Beth, though, going into Crackers & Crates in the company of another woman and couldn't help but wonder if she knew of Michael Parish's presence, or, if she didn't, what I might read from her reaction when she learned of it. Reluctant as I was to deal with her, I went in pursuit.

She was at the counter, waiting for a clerk to expedite her order. I didn't see the other woman. I stood next to Beth. As if she sensed my presence, she turned to me with her please-state-your-business look.

"What do you want, Cleary?"

"I was hoping you could bring me up to date," I said. "One day this place isn't for sale and never will be, for any price. The next day, news breaks of the coming of a Japanese businessman with deep pockets because the Parishes may be — how did you put it? — 'ready to deal.'"

Beth squinted at me with hard suspicion.

"And now with Michael Parish in town, in fact staying right here at the Inn..."

Bingo. Agitated surprise flashed across her face, after which her effort to mask it was visible.

"Forgive me for being slow," I said, "but this is more than a simple guy like me can keep track of."

Evidence of my obtuseness brought her back to a position of superiority.

"You seem to have trouble figuring out what's going on right under your nose," she said.

I looked at her with as much significance as I could muster and said, "An old problem of mine."

The other woman I had seen stepped out from an aisle and came to her side. It was Beth's mother!

I hadn't seen Henrietta since some time before the breakup. She was exactly as I remembered her — expensively dressed and coiffed, decked out in precious metals and gems, on the lookout for something or someone to disdain. Lucky me.

When Beth and I were married, she would visit us once or twice a year — inspection tours, I came to think of them — managing in those visits to make me feel unwelcome in my own home, a home at which she turned up her patrician nose for being too small and too common. I suspect she had never forgiven me, and maybe Beth too, for our unannounced and unceremonious wedding before she had the opportunity to meet and disapprove of me.

"Well, well," I said. "No one told me it was Mother-Daughter Day at the mall."

The clerk gave Beth her order in a paper bag. She paid and pursed her change.

Henrietta held her glasses down her nose by one corner and inspected me over the top of them. She curled her mouth in distaste.

"Elizabeth," she said, looking me up and down, "tell this unfortunate creature to go away."

The son of a coal miner who carried black dust home on his clothes, in the pores of his skin, enough of it in his lungs eventually to kill him, I have always been sensitive to imperious classism of the kind Henrietta gave off. It occurred to me as she spoke that I was in her presence for the first time with no obligation to treat her with deference and no domestic consequences to face if I didn't.

I smiled as I browsed a mental catalog of insults, any one of which had the potential for turning Henrietta's cool contempt into hot indignation. I must have all but licked my chops, for Beth flushed and Henrietta seemed to brace herself, as if for a blow. Unless the dynamic between them had changed, I knew Beth wouldn't be entirely displeased to witness her mother's comeuppance.

We stood for a moment in a triangle wired for vengeful, retributive current. I saw myself reflected in a large gold bangle at Henrietta's throat.

"I'll save you the trouble," I said to Beth, and walked off. I hadn't learned anything tangible, but Beth's reaction to hearing of Michael Parish's presence was telling enough.

As for Henrietta, if I was gentler with her than I might have been, it was because, when it comes to classism, I don't stand entirely outside the circle of culpability. Truth be told, I tend to look down on those above me.

CHAPTER 28
FELICITY PARISH

In the days following Michael Parish's arrival, I saw him twice. The first time was on a night near closing time. I was checking doors in a service corridor on the lower level of the mall that ran all the way to the basement of the Inn. In the distant semi-dark, Michael Parish stood with Rudy Westphal. He appeared to be haranguing him. Slumped and with his head down, Rudy looked despondent. It seemed an odd pairing at an odd time in an odd place.

Rudy, whom I knew only by name, had always struck me as mildly strange and skittish. He looked to be in his sixties, and I had assumed from his attire that he worked in some maintenance capacity at the hotel. Seeing him with Michael Parish that night made me wonder if he might be one of the "family staff," referred to in the *Vanity Fair* piece, that cared for Felicity Parish.

The next day, around noon, I went to the Inn desk to pilfer newspapers. I took a chair and hid behind the *News-Gazette* with both ears cocked and one eye periscoped. A maid with a cart full of cleaning supplies and sheets and towels got on an elevator. A bellhop passed through. Felix, per his custom, was taking lunch in the office behind the desk, ready to spring into view if someone hit the bell. Then the elderly gentleman I knew only as Thomas came pushing a cart with a meal under a glass dome, with sterling silver and fine china.

He stopped and reached around a square pillar at the far end of the desk and produced a clipboard. He checked something off, rehung the clipboard, and took the elevator up.

Thomas had been at the Inn for at least as long as I had worked at the mall, but I never knew in what capacity. I might have once supposed he was a bell captain, but I had never seen him lift a bag for a guest. He was gray, trim, and desiccate, wintry-eyed, arch, and distant. In spite of our having worked within sight of each other for so long, we had never exchanged so much as a nod, thanks to a talent he had for making me feel invisible. After he got on the elevator, no one was about.

I went to that pillar at the far end of the desk, removed the clipboard Thomas had consulted, and returned to the chair with it and held it behind the open newspaper.

Clipped together was a stack of identical checklists, each with MISS PARISH centered at the top and a blank line for the date in the top-right corner. Running down the page, with a designated time for each item, was an exhaustive list of daily requirements: meals, tea, medicines, linen changes, laundry. It seemed that if she chose, Miss Parish would never have to leave her rooms.

I replaced the clipboard on its hook and returned to the mall.

The next morning I went to the U of I Library. Guessing at the year, I started with the 1938 indexes to both the *New York Times* and *Chicago Tribune*. The *Trib* had no entries on Felicity Parish, the Times only one. The abstract indicated that it was a review of a Broadway musical in which she had appeared in a supporting role.

The abstracted entries in both indexes for 1939 and 1940 indicated a career on the rise. She progressed from supporting roles to leads on stage and in films and worked with Spencer Tracy and Cary Grant, among other leading men. In January of 1941 she married John Nash, a naval officer from "a good family in the East," after which she appeared in a couple of more films. There was nothing on what might have happened to her at Pearl Harbor. 1942 contained no references under her name. I checked the rest of the 1940s and found nothing.

Only one of the earlier entries indicated that the article referenced included a photo. I went to the microfilm cabinets, found the right one, and set it up on a machine. It wasn't a posed promotional shot, rather a scene from the movie under review; it was grainy and poorly lit, and Felicity Parish stood at such an oblique angle that I couldn't get a good read on her face.

I returned to the indexes, hoping to learn more. The 1950s had nothing. I came close to giving up, but decided to try the 1960s. Sure enough, the *Trib* ran a piece on her in early December of 1966, a whatever-happened-to story as a sidebar to a feature on the twenty-fifth anniversary of the Japanese attack on Pearl Harbor.

Back in microfilms, I found and set up the edition of the *Trib* with the article, rotated the wheel until I came to the piece, which contained a photo, and learned the following:

Her husband had been granted leave upon their marriage, and they honeymooned in Hawaii. After that, they settled in San Diego, where he was stationed. She retained her last name and continued to work for a while under studio contract.

In late May she learned that she was pregnant. In July, her husband was transferred to Hawaii, which they had grown to love on their honeymoon and to which they had vowed someday to return. As a service couple, they couldn't live in the luxury to which they were both accustomed, but at least they would be stationed in what they had come to think of as the closest thing on earth to paradise.

They made the move and set up house on Ford Island. The rest of the world might have been sliding into madness and destruction, but Felicity and her husband were too much in love and too happily anticipating parenthood to notice.

On Sunday morning, December 7, with her husband on duty aboard the USS Arizona on Battleship Row, Felicity was alone in their apartment, perhaps waking up over a cup of tea, when the first wave of Japanese planes descended upon Oahu.

(The author admitted at this point that some of what followed was speculation on his part, given the Parish family's fierce protection of its privacy.)

Unnerved by the attack, when Felicity later received news that her husband was certainly dead, she collapsed.

For the next several weeks she was an almost complete mental and physical wreck. In early February, her doctor induced labor and delivered a stillborn baby boy. With that, she seemed to have lost whatever rational faculties she might have retained. Her father gave the dead child the name John and ordered cremation.

She may have spent the next year in the psychiatric ward of a hospital. In early 1943 she was under care at the family compound in Lake Forest, Illinois, having regained enough mental and physical capacity to attend to her own bodily processes, but a broken woman in heart, mind, and spirit.

At this point the trajectory of her life grew even dimmer. The author guessed that she stayed in Lake Forest in a state of almost total dementia until about 1964 or 1965, at which time, having become a pawn in the family squabble, she was relocated. All that was known for certain was that she never resurfaced in public. Inquiries by the press and her erstwhile fans into her whereabouts and welfare were rebuffed.

I rotated the wheel back to the photo. It was more than forty years old, and, like the one I had seen earlier, it was dark and grainy. But the angle was better, a frontal view of her face. She stood peering down at the camera with one eyebrow arched, part vamp, part dominatrix. The regal air might have been intended to compensate for ordinary looks. I studied that face a while longer, trying to imagine it after more than forty years and much trauma.

I had entered the library on a bright but blustery Friday morning. By the time I left, leaden clouds had gathered overhead, apt symbols of what I feared might be afoot.

Satoshi Matsuta was due in town that evening. On Saturday morning he was to be taken on a guided tour of the mall so that he might determine if his employer, which years before had contributed in oblique fashion to the undoing of Felicity Parish, should help finance Roger Worthington's dream of turning Lincoln Inn and Lincoln Court, Felicity Parish's last refuge, into Lincoln Center. I had the ominous feeling that that dream would be realized over more dead bodies than the two that had already been hauled out of the place.

Mightily curious, most mightily wary that the murderous business that began with the deaths of Joe Whitehead and Martha Herrera wasn't yet finished, I set out on foot across campus toward the mall.

CHAPTER 29
THE GENTLEMAN FROM JAPAN

My second sighting of Michael Parish came on the day of Matsuta's tour of Lincoln Court, the Saturday morning before Christmas.

Bob and the rest of the maintenance crew had been sprucing the place up. With Christmas decorations hung and virtually every item of merchandise in every store on deep discount, Matsuta would be seeing Lincoln Court at its busiest and in its most festive light.

At ten o'clock, Beth and Matsuta came down from the Inn lobby. He was young, trim, and handsome in a dark blue suit. She wore black pants and a charcoal blazer over a red blouse buttoned to the throat.

I started out keeping an eye on them from the monitor room, on the screens and through the windows. When Michael Parish emerged from the Inn a few minutes later, I went down to be closer to the action.

Beth and Matsuta went into stores and talked with managers and clerks. Beth had on her sales face, between the seams of which I thought I could detect hints of strain. That might have been because she was aware that Michael Parish was somewhere on the scene, but I imagined, too, her walking the line between the probability that Matsuta had heard about the murders and the hope that he hadn't.

Michael Parish meandered around. If he was following them, he was being discreet, for they never crossed paths. I didn't know if Beth would have recognized him if they had. At one point Rudy made a pass through the mall, casting nervous looks about.

Roger Worthington joined Beth and Matsuta for lunch at the Inn around twelve thirty, after which they all went up to Worthington's office. I resisted the temptation to try eavesdropping from the monitor room.

A couple of hours later they came out. Beth escorted her guest to the top of the steps that led from the terrace to the Inn lobby, where they parted company. I got off at six o'clock and decided not to hang around.

I spent that night in my apartment alternately telling myself that I was being paranoid to think that murder was afoot at Lincoln Court or Lincoln Inn and reminding myself that two murders had already been committed there.

On Sunday morning at ten thirty I showed up half expecting to hear that Matsuta had been dispatched in his room overnight. I helped myself to fat Sunday editions of the *Trib* and *News-Gazette* at the Inn desk and joined Leo on the terrace. The walkers walked and chattered. The Brethren came up from their services. Alice, with her shopping bag, muttered to herself on a bench. I didn't see Michael Parish anywhere. Rudy made another pass through, again looking like he was wound tight. Eleven o'clock came, and the security grates on the stores went up.

Matsuta, very much alive, appeared at the top of the stairs. He went through the terrace into the mall. No one accompanied him and no one met him. Perhaps he had asked for time to experience the place unmediated by sales talk. He did a slow circuit of the entire perimeter then went into Craddock's, where I lost sight of him.

I waited a few minutes then left the terrace and took the stairs down and entered Craddock's on the lower level. Keeping a weather eye, I pretended to be interested in what was left of kitchen wares, then decided to take Craddock's elevator to the top floor and check things out as I worked my way back down.

The elevator doors opened. Matsuta sat in a corner, his face deathly pale and fixed in a grimace, eyes open and staring at eternity. Blood smeared the wall behind him and spread in a puddle on the floor.

I got on.

Some things you know. I knew he was dead. The doors closed behind me and the car rose. As it did, Matsuta slumped over on his side. The handle of what appeared to be a large kitchen knife stuck out of his back. Given its placement, and inferring the blade size from the handle, I guessed that it might have gone through his heart.

I was kneeling over the body when the elevator stopped. It occurred to me that anyone on the other side of the doors might take me for a murderer, but it was too late to do anything about it. I rose and turned as the doors opened onto the top floor of Craddock's.

A female customer stood there. I stepped into the space between the elevator doors.

"You don't want to get on," I said.

She looked around me, put a hand to her mouth, drew in a sharp breath, and rushed off. The doors closed on my shoulders and reopened as I stood and thought, did so again, then again. I felt like the object of an industrial process. The next time the doors opened I hurried to a nearby chair, the one the husband sits in while the wife shops, carried it back, and set it where I had stood.

A clerk watched from what she might have thought to be a safe distance. The customer had retreated behind her to a safe distance from me. I went to them and told the clerk to call the police.

Despite the day and hour, Harold Bivins was among the cops who showed up ten minutes later. I filled him in. He screwed up his face at me and said, "What is it with you?"

CHAPTER 30
FRAN

Bivins's question struck me as nothing more than an offhand remark on the coincidence of my being more or less present at the murders of both Joe Whitehead and Satoshi Matsuta. After I got to the mall on Monday morning it became clear that, no matter what he meant at the time, the question had stuck in his craw.

A couple of cops in uniform, notepads in hand, worked the concourses. One of them came to me.

"The chief is down in the Community Room. He wants to see you."

Bivins had gone on to question me, albeit superficially, at the scene the day before, so I was unsure what this was about. I expected to find him there with Ken Lakis and wondered if Lakis would attempt to drive the square peg of Matsuta's killing into the round hole of his mob conspiracy theory or dismiss it as unrelated. Bivins was alone, pacing at one end of the room and looking out of sorts.

"Where's our friend from Springfield?" I said.

He waved a hand. "In Springfield."

Without going into detail, he explained that Lakis's case against Richie Miranda had unraveled and that instead of admitting it and moving in another direction, Lakis had dumped it into the state's attorney's lap, declared victory and gone home.

He told me to sit. I sat. He didn't offer me coffee. He continued to pace and looked at me through narrowed eyes.

"We couldn't get a clear set of fingerprints from the knife that killed Matsuta," he said, impatience and frustration in his voice. "We have no clues or leads." It sounded like an accusation.

"Do you want me to confess?"

He snapped at me. "That would actually help a lot. You make me wish there was a law against being a wise guy." He was clearly out of patience and, with his job perhaps on the line, maybe feeling like he was running out of time.

He said he had grilled Karl Thomaczek, having caught wind of his threatening talk before Matsuta's arrival. I suppose he had to, but Karl struck me as cherishing his hatred too much to quench it. "It turns out he was cooling off in the hospital at the time of the murder," Bivins said. "He got so worked up that his blood pressure went off the charts."

Bivins didn't mention Michael Parish, nor did he hint at any connection between the murders and the Parish family. I didn't share my growing suspicion along those lines or what I had learned about Felicity Parish.

I suppose by then my carrying around that death threat against Whitehead had made me secretive, and wary that I might be open to a charge of obstructing justice. Maybe too I had grown attached to the idea of solving what the cops couldn't. Whatever the reason, I sat there thinking that Bivins wasn't asking the right questions and that I wasn't inclined to help him discover them.

Bivins finally let me go, but I knew he wasn't satisfied.

I went upstairs. When I passed Music! Music! Fran Piper summoned me with a wave. I went to her, hoping she didn't have another shoplifter for me to bust.

"What's up, good looking?" I said.

Fran blushed, then composed herself.

"This probably isn't important," she said. "But in case it is... It happened several weeks ago. I guess I should have said something earlier, but I didn't think much of it at the time. But it was strange, and with all the spooky stuff going on around here, I mean those murders, maybe there's a connection. And now with that Japanese guy getting stabbed to death yesterday, I figured maybe I should say something, and since you're with security and I feel okay talking to you and..."

"Tell me what happened, Fran."

"It was this time I was in the bathroom in the basement. It was weeks ago, like I say, maybe even before those two people were murdered at the Inn." She thought a moment then nodded with certainty. "Yes, it was before. I was in one of the stalls, and like, you know, doing my business." She blushed again. "I can't believe I'm telling you this. It was a little after five o'clock and nobody was around, customers I mean. Not like there ever are. Anyway, somebody came in the bathroom while I was in there and walked through. Then I heard what sounded like a key in a lock. Then a door opened and shut. From the sound I could tell it was the door on the far wall. I use that bathroom all the time, and I guess I always assumed that door was to a storage closet or something. Then I heard it being locked from the other side."

"Then what?"

"Then nothing. Somebody came in, walked by and went through that door, then closed it and locked it behind them. When I came out of the stall nobody else was around, and I went to that door and tried it. It was locked."

"How many stalls are there, and which one were you in?"

"Two, but one has an out-of-order sign on it and the door doesn't latch on the other, the one I was in. The hardware's broken, and the door rests open a few inches if you don't hold it shut, which you can't exactly do and do your business at the same time." She clucked and shook her head. "Maintenance around this place — I swear."

"Are you saying you got a look at who passed through?"

"No, I had my head down. I mean if whoever it was saw me, I didn't want to see them seeing me. Know what I mean? But it occurred to me later that maybe the person didn't see me either. With the stall door open a few inches it might have looked like the place was empty."

"And no one else was in the bathroom?"

"No. Anyway, it struck me as strange, somebody coming in and then going through that door. Maybe it's no big deal, but I thought I'd mention it just in case, with everything that's been going on."

"Have you told this to the cops or anyone else?"

"Are you kidding? I'm embarrassed enough telling you. I'm hoping you won't mention it to anyone, or at least not use my name if you do."

"Your secret's good with me, Fran," I said.

CHAPTER 31
THE LADIES ROOM

After my conversation with Fran, I went downstairs to look for the back side of the door she had heard someone go through. The bathroom was on the basement level of the Inn, in a hall that ran under it and connected to the mall. Past the front entrance to it was a narrow service corridor that led to an even narrower passageway that dead-ended at a floor-to-ceiling plywood partition, painted to match the walls. According to my mental map, the door should have been on the other side of that partition, but there was no way through. I decided to try another tack.

I waited until four o'clock, when I knew Helen Jefferson, a favorite of mine at the mall, would be cleaning that rest room and the men's room near it. When I went down, Helen's cart stood nearby. No one was in the men's room. I opened the door to the women's and peeked in. Helen was scrubbing sinks. I walked in as if I had every right to be there.

"Hi, Helen," I said. "Are you the only one here?"

She stood up from her work and stared at me dumbfounded.

"Boy, what on earth you doing here?"

"Tracking a killer. And you might be able to help."

She shook her head and resumed scrubbing, hoping I would go away if I ignored me.

"That door there," I said, pointing to the one on the far wall, "is that a supply closet?"

"Ain't no supplies in there," she said. "I don't know what that door is for."

"Would you mind seeing if you can open it with one of your keys?"

She made a face and shook her head but left off scrubbing. She wiped her hands on her apron, fished a ring of keys from a pocket and tried some.

"There, if any work it'd be one of these right here, and none of 'em does." She picked up her cleaning sponge again and shook it at me. "Now you git from here."

I tried keys from my set. None fit.

"I have a favor to ask, Helen," I said. She eyed me with suspicion. "I know this is out of line, but if you'd be so kind as to go into the stall on the end there and sit as if you were doing your business."

"Boy, have you lost your mind?"

"Trust me." I ushered her by the elbow into the stall that Fran said she had used. "Just have a seat. And let the door rest open."

She tisked and shook her head in exasperation but obliged me. I went back to the entrance and took in the scene, then walked to the door in the far wall. For all I could see, the stall Helen was in might have been empty.

"You can come out now, Helen."

"You done bein' foolish?" she said as she emerged.

Above that inner door a metal cylinder with lens-like glass at the end was mounted to the wall behind a wire-mesh cage.

"Is that an emergency light?" I said, pointing.

Helen had gone back to scrubbing. "I got no idea," she said without looking up from her work.

"Thanks, Helen. I owe you."

She shook her head as I went to the door to leave.

On my way out I almost collided with Beth on her way in. She regarded me as if I had jumped out of ambush with an upraised spear.

I held the door open. As much as the space allowed, Beth circled away from me as she went in, never taking her eyes off me.

What I'd have given at that moment for some scatological zinger so cutting as to cause Beth to fill her pants before she could get into a stall and get them down. Alas, nothing came.

CHAPTER 32
LEO

I had a hunch, but before testing its weight out on the end of a limb I wanted to consult with Leo.

Trim and wiry, square-jawed and flinty-eyed, Leo drove to Lincoln Court every morning in his Cadillac. He spent part of his time on the Terrace with black coffee and newspapers, the ones I pilfered from the Inn desk, the rest of it visiting the attractive young and not-so-young women who worked at the mall. To my knowledge he never made inappropriate verbal or physical advances to them. He seemed content to be near them, to smell them, to hear their voices, to see the tender swell of their breasts under sweater or blouse. Most of them either genuinely enjoyed his company or were at least willing to humor him. Those who disdained him he left alone. He was also a film buff, whose eye for the ladies extended to silver screen beauties, past and present. I was curious to know how much he knew about Felicity Parish.

On the morning after my visit to the women's restroom, we were at our table on the terrace. I told him what I had learned about Felicity Parish and her family, omitting any mention of my having seen Michael Parish on the premises.

"It could be a movie script," I said. "Young female star with the world at her fingertips suffers tragic loss of husband, child, mental faculties, and ends up a recluse, right here in our midst, cared for by her own private staff."

With what amounted to a shrug, Leo said he had heard the rumors about her presence at the Inn. I gathered he hadn't been a fan of hers.

"I've seen her in one or two films on The Late Show," Leo said. "I never quite understood her appeal. Okay looking, I guess, but no beauty, and not the kind that ages well. Too goggle-eyed for my taste."

"So you don't come to Lincoln Court for a glimpse of the once-famous starlet?"

"What glimpse?" Leo said. "They say she never leaves her rooms. Funny you should ask, though."

"Why's that?"

"Maybe you wasn't here at the time, but some of the girls said there was an Urbana cop nosing around yesterday asking about Felicity Parish."

CHAPTER 33
GUNFIRE

I was in Schwartz's bookstore on the afternoon of that same day when the shooting started. Somewhere on the upper level, glass broke and fell to the floor. A second shot had the same effect. A third ricocheted. The few people out on the concourse scrambled for cover. I hunkered down where I was, between shelves to the right of the center aisle.

My first thought was of Brazelton. He had declared personal war on Omega, the pigeon, after it dive-bombed him a couple of times, and I figured he had finally boiled over and gone gunning for it. The shots seemed to be coming from the balcony above and across from the bookstore. When most of a minute had passed since the last one, I crawled down an outer aisle toward the front then moved between Westerns and Mysteries toward the center. Another shot cracked the silence and broke another window. Whoever was doing the shooting seemed interested more in ventilating the place than in targeting people.

I was still too far back in the store to see up to the balcony, so I scrambled to the next aisle and took refuge between Philosophy and Religion. On the other side of the center aisle a whale of a woman quivered and sobbed on the floor between Romance and Self-Improvement. She looked over, saw me, and shrieked.

I moved forward again. I went out and crossed the concourse to the stairs and began a slow, cautious ascent. At eye level with the balcony I flattened against the top few steps, stuck my head into the walkway and looked left and right. I didn't see anyone. I went on up, and on a hunch, turned left. Further down, Rudy Westphal sat on the floor against a wall of an alcove with electrical and utility closets. At first I thought he might have taken cover there, then I spotted a handgun next to him on the floor. It was a straight shot from where he sat to the broken windows in the roof.

"What's wrong, Rudy?" I asked.

He looked straight ahead. "Only everything," he said.

The cops arrived down on the concourse. I extended my foot and scooted the gun away out of Rudy's reach then went to the railing and waved and yelled down to them.

CHAPTER 34
RUDY

The next day's *News-Gazette* reported that Rudy Westphal had confessed to the murders of Joe Whitehead, Martha Herrera, and Satoshi Matsuta, insisting that he had acted alone and on his own behalf. There was no mention of motive.

I didn't believe it for a minute. I doubted the cops believed it either, but since Lakis's return to Springfield, they had been casting about for culprits, and I found it easy to imagine that they might accept Rudy's confession at face value and allow him to take the rap.

Aside from that confession, the reports that emerged in the next twenty-four hours had him uncooperative and tight-lipped, with nothing to say about himself or his supposed motives. The newspaper listed both his residence and his employer as Lincoln Inn. He either couldn't make bail or declined to, and no one made it for him.

Rudy's plight aroused my curiosity, and a certain amount of sympathy. I had a hunch that he had acted to divert attention from someone and that that someone might allow him to twist alone in the wind. On an afternoon off from work I decided to pay him a visit. He seemed surprised and puzzled at my coming, and yet, if I read him right, also grateful. We sat opposite each other at a table. A guard stood nearby.

"Who killed the people you say you killed, Rudy?" I said.

He insisted he had, but was entirely unconvincing.

"I had my reasons," was all he would say when I asked him why.

When I told him I had seen him with Michael Parish in that service corridor, he denied knowledge of any such person and that any such meeting had taken place. "You must have mistaken somebody else for me," he said with a vigorous shake of his head. At my mention of the feud between Michael Parish and his half-siblings and the implications of that feud for the future of the Inn and the Court and for Felicity Parish, his countenance registered sadness, anger and desperation.

"We only wanted to be left alone," he said.

We?

He clammed up, refused to explain or comment further, and asked the guard to escort me out.

I had the feeling that Rudy had come to the pathetic awareness that his life had meaning only in terms of its being a minor chapter in the life of someone else, and that that chapter had come to a close.

"Who's using you, Rudy?" I said as I rose to leave.

He closed his eyes and lowered his face into his hands, as if to cry or to pray.

As I went down the steps from the building, Thomas approached on foot through falling snow. I thought of waiting and confronting him, with what fact or accusation I couldn't say, but so grim, gray, and chilling was his aspect that I couldn't bring myself to do so. I headed off in the opposite direction. When I looked back, he was ascending the steps to the jail.

The next day I learned that sometime in the night Rudy had hanged himself in his cell.

All the rest of that day, I was haunted by images of Rudy — slumped while being harangued by Michael Parish, sitting forlornly on the floor of the balcony next to the gun, his head in his hands in the jail as I left him, and one more that hadn't quite registered at the moment.

As I waited for the cops to come up to the balcony after I found Rudy, he had got to his feet and came over and stood next to me at the rail. Moments later, while he was being handcuffed, I saw dirt on a couple of fingers of one hand, not ground in, but fresh and moist.

I returned to that spot on the balcony. Planter boxes with ivy hung by brackets from the railing. In one, a small patch of dirt looked blacker than the rest, as if it had been recently disturbed. I stuck two fingers in and probed. They touched cool metal. I pulled out a key.

CHAPTER 35
FOREVER YOUNG

My talk with Leo had left me less certain about my hunch but no less determined to act on it. But my plan would work under only one circumstance, and all day Christmas Eve that circumstance never materialized.

In anticipation of a crush of last-minute shoppers, Wendell, Brazelton, and I and a couple of temps hired for the occasion were on duty from open to close. Art, seeming to think he could *worry* dollars out of customers, had been putting in overtime the last several days and was on the scene too. That made me uneasy, but when around six o'clock I saw what I needed to see, I decided to have a go at it anyway.

I went out the north end and walked a block east to make a call from a pay phone at a gas station, then returned to the mall and entered the east end. Brazelton was there, herding customers and clerks out the door.

"Make yourself useful," he groused. "We just got a damn bomb threat."

Under the pretext of following his order, I moved to the hub, from where I had a view down all four concourses. Wendell was ushering people out the west exit; one of the temps did the same at the north one. I went to a service corridor off the south concourse, followed that to a set of stairs in a corner of the hotel and took them up to the top floor.

I found my way to room 712, the number stamped on the key I had found in the planter. No one was about. I put the key in the lock and tried it. It turned a bolt.

I walked into what might have been a living room, except the look and smell of it had more to do with dying. Dim blue-gray light from somewhere filled the space. Heavy curtains covered the windows. Dust and cobwebs were everywhere. I felt like Pip at Miss Havisham's place. From within a large gilt frame on one wall, Felicity Parish stood regal in a floor-length evening gown in an enlargement of the same picture I had seen on microfilm at the library. She looked down at the camera — down at *me* — one eyebrow imperiously arched. Under it a cabinet held a television and videotape player.

I turned and looked up and saw the source of the light: Mounted high on another wall, television monitors showed live black-and-white views of Lincoln Court, including the interior of the women's restroom in the basement that I had recently visited. On one, Art hustled about; he appeared to be giving orders to Wendell and Brazelton. On separate monitors I saw them go to the exits. Clerks and customers began drifting back in, much too soon for a thorough bomb search to have been conducted.

I snooped and poked around and looked behind the curtains, all the while wondering if I might be appearing on a monitor somewhere. On a dusty tabletop was a stack of glossy photos, posed and candid shots and scenes from films, all of Felicity Parish, including a copy of the one on the wall. On a shelf under the television was a collection of videotapes, stacked on edge and labeled. I took one with the title *Forever Young* on it, put it in the tape player, set it to running and turned on the TV. Music played as credits rolled, among them

FELICITY PARISH... as DIANE

As the music faded, a young woman in a calf-length skirt, curls bouncing under a hat trimmed with lace, went through a gate in a picket fence in front of a cottage. On the porch a man in suspenders took a pipe from his mouth and waited to greet her with a smile and open arms.

How was my girl's first day at work? he said as she went up the steps.

She permitted herself to be hugged, then said, *Daddy, I don't understand men.*

I muted the volume and went down a hall and into a bathroom, using the penlight I had used when I broke into Roger Worthington's office. A mirrorless medicine cabinet held pills, salves, and ointments. From there I went into a bedroom.

Black cloth covered a vanity mirror. I opened the drawers of a bedside table; they were full of bottles of pills, including what appeared to be a large supply of Seconal. A low chest sat at the foot of a disheveled bed. I lifted the lid to find a vintage collection of dresses from about the 1930s and '40s, each folded neatly in its own cellophane bag.

On the vanity, mixed with cosmetics, were scraps and full sheets of stationery of a weight, color, and grade that matched the stuff that the death threat against Whitehead had been written on. Some bore scribbled ramblings. I took the sheet from my sport coat pocket and put it with the others.

Concerned that my time was running short, I went back into the living room, intending to leave. A clunking noise came from a corner. I stepped back into the hall and stood out of sight and heard what sounded like a set of elevator doors slide open then close. Floorboards creaked. Paper crinkled. Too late, I remembered that the television was still on, the tape still running. I considered but dismissed the idea of hiding until I might escape undetected, then stepped back into the living room.

She saw me and dropped her shopping bag.

"Hi, Alice," I said. "Which is Wonderland, up here or downstairs?"

CHAPTER 36
HER MAJESTY

The transformation she underwent in the next few seconds was startling. She arched an eyebrow, puckered her mouth, flared her nostrils, stood upright with shoulders back. She lifted her chin, stretching tight the wattle at her throat. In spite of my considerable height advantage, she managed to look *down* at me, cool and imperious. Even her clothes seemed of finer stuff.

"One of us is lost," she said in a modulated version of her downstairs voice.

"Which one?" I asked. "Alice or Felicity?"

She blinked and squinted and seemed to slump, as if the effort required to assume her other identity had overtaxed her, then went to a tattered wing chair and plopped wearily down. She gestured with a shaky finger to a matching chair opposite and said, "Sit, Mr. Cleary."

I obeyed.

She looked at me, her head bobbling, and said, "Are you aware that there has been a bomb threat?"

"Inasmuch as I phoned it in, yes I am."

She smiled. "Perhaps Mr. Ziemann knows that. We weren't outside five minutes before he came to assure us that all was safe."

Good old Art. It seemed that for the sake of business he had taken the chance that the call was a hoax. Perhaps too he had seen or been told of my movements and knew where it came from. If so, I'd be going back down jobless and in trouble with the law.

"You know my name," I said.

"This is my place," she said. "I make a point of knowing what goes on here."

"And a nice setup it is," I said. "Private surveillance. Secret ways of coming and going. I'm reminded of stories in which the queen goes about in disguise among her subjects."

She at first smiled, then seemed to grow confused.

"Why are you here?" she asked in a voice part Felicity's, part Alice's, as if she stood astride the chasm that separated her two selves.

"To confirm my suspicions about who murdered Joe Whitehead, Martha Herrera, and Satoshi Matsuta. No doubt you're behind it all, but I can't help wondering who did the dirty work. Rudy? Thomas? Your brother Michael? I suppose I shouldn't rule you out, especially in Matsuta's case."

The bony fingers of one hand fluttered to her chest like a bird taking flight against the wind, and her face took on the look of wounded innocence.

"What a horrid thing to think a girl might do," she said.

"I suppose so," I said, then added a calculated fillip: "Not to mention difficult, given your age and infirmity."

Affronted, she summoned energy from somewhere and, entirely Felicity again, said, "You are in my apartment uninvited, making accusations you can't prove. Must I call the police?"

"Go ahead," I said. "You'd be saving me the trouble."

I had no sooner spoken than I had second thoughts. If she did call the police, police whose motives and professional abilities I questioned, she could tell them, among other things, that I had broken into her place and had admitted to having called in a bomb threat to the mall. It occurred to me, too, that inasmuch as I was making life difficult for an impaired old woman on Christmas Eve, I might not come off as the sympathetic character in this drama.

A spider moved across the floor, and it came to me with chilling clarity that I was alone in the company of someone directly or indirectly responsible for multiple murders and who probably considered me little more than a bothersome member of the underclass, perhaps as much a threat to her position as those she had had murdered. For all I knew she had already pressed a button to summon Thomas or someone else to dispatch me on the spot. No one knew I was there, so no one would be the wiser. Nor would I be mourned by any living person I could think of.

She turned her attention to the television and smiled with a kind of rapt nostalgia as "Diane" looked adoringly up and into the eyes of the young man who held her in his arms.

"This is where he tells me he will love me forever," she said.

We were sitting near one of the heavy curtains I had looked behind before she came. I stood and pushed it to one side, revealing plate glass next to a door that led onto a balcony.

"Take a look at forever, *old woman*."

As I had hoped and suspected, the light from the television and security monitors overhead combined with the dark outside to turn the window into a mirror. At first in surprise, then in dread and awe, she regarded her ravaged, waxen reflection. She blinked and gaped and seemed to struggle for breath. She slumped in the chair, dropped her chin to her chest, raised it again. She opened her mouth. What came out was a faint squawk in Alice's timbre. On the television screen, "Diane," aglow with happiness, primped in front of a mirror.

To this day I feel discomfiture at recalling what happened next.

Thinking to position myself for an exit, I had moved to the center of the room and was looking back and forth from her in the chair to her on the television screen to her reflection in the window, when I was startled to see a man in the glass with a menacing frown. He seemed to be either reflected from behind me or standing out on the balcony, and for a moment I was sure that by some secret means she had summoned my assassin and that he had arrived. I spun around in alarm, but no one was there. When I turned back around, the man turned too, and I realized that that dour, middle-aged man in the glass, whirling like some ridiculous marionette, was me.

Alice's squawky voice brought me back to myself. "What do you intend to do?"

Had she asked at some moment other than that one, and had I stronger principles regarding justice and the law in general and less equivocal feelings about this case in particular, the answer to that question might have been clear. But it wasn't. I was preoccupied, too, by the specter of that frown on my face reflecting back at me. To another man wearing such a frown I'd have attributed a meanness of spirit of which I would have thought myself incapable. Yet there I was, making life miserable for an infirm old woman who had suffered the loss of her husband and the child in her womb in a national calamity, the resultant loss of her career and her faculties, the rejection of most of her family, certain members of which might be willing to sacrifice her to fatten their bottom line.

"I'll go through that door," I said, indicating the one I had come through into her apartment. "After that, I don't know."

I went to the door and looked back. Bent forward in the chair, Felicity Parish was a picture of misery and graceless old age.

"There is one thing I'm curious about," I said. "Why didn't you go after Roger Worthington?"

She looked over at me and through a pathetic, crooked smile said, "He amuses us."

CHAPTER 37
SPINNING AROUND THE SUN

I stepped into the hall with the intention of retracing the route that had brought me there. I went right, but when I reached a T intersection I couldn't remember which direction I had come from. I went right again and proceeded until I came to a long hall that went off to the left. As I was thinking that I might have stumbled into Wonderland indeed, Thomas came around the corner at the other end.

He saw me, hesitated a moment, then came my way, picking up his pace. I reversed directions, Thomas's persistent footfall behind me. The hair on the back of my neck bristled.

I turned a corner, passed room 712, turned left and came to an exit sign. I went through the door. Concrete steps led only up. I took them. At the top was a metal door with a small, mesh-reinforced window through which I could see stars. I tried some keys from my ring, but none fit. I tried the knob. The door was unlocked. I went through.

The edge of the roof lay a few steps ahead, beyond and below it the east parking lot. A Salvation Army bell and the cheerful voices of what sounded like a young couple drifted up through the clear, cold air. I looked back, expecting Thomas to come through the door, but he didn't.

Behind me on the roof, vapor rose from pipes, and machinery hummed and purred. The building felt like some great sleeping beast that might awaken at any moment and swallow me whole.

Vapor from my breath blew off toward the stars. Wispy clouds raced toward Orion, ascending the southeastern sky; near the horizon lay what could have been his bow, the thin crescent of a waning, tobacco-stained moon.

For the first time in many years, I recalled the solitary game I took to playing around the age of fourteen, following the death of my father. After learning in geometry class that any three nonaligned points — *any* three — form a triangle, I'd sneak outside on clear nights when I was supposed to be in bed — winter nights like this one were especially thrilling — and imagine lines connecting pairs of stars, intersected at their ends by lines connecting those stars to me. Dizzy and reeling, I'd stand for long stretches at one vertex of an immense celestial triangle until I was scolded back into the house or grew too cold or too sleepy to endure longer.

There on the Inn roof, spinning around the sun with Beth and Steve, Roger Worthington, the Brethren, Joe Whitehead and Martha Herrera and Satoshi Matsuta and Rudy in or on the way to their graves or the furnace's fire, Felicity Parish — the entire ridiculous dead and dying lot of us — I fell into a variation on that game, triangulating with Sirius and, somehow, myself at fourteen, from whom I felt more distant than from the stars.

With no taste for going back down through the hotel, I walked across the roof to the fire escape stairs on its south face and took them down. As my feet hit the pavement, I saw Thomas hurrying across the parking lot with a small piece of black luggage. He got in a car and drove off.

EPILOGUE
OMEGA

"According to this," Leo said from behind the front section of the Sunday *News-Gazette*, "Brazelton got off light — a fine, probation, and an order to go for counseling."

"Not to mention loss of job," I said.

Leo lowered his paper. "What was that nut case thinking?"

"He was gunning for the pigeon," I said. "He'd been threatening to for weeks. When it crapped on him — the day after he lost his shirt betting on the Super Bowl, as I understand it — he went home, came back with a gun, and opened fire."

Out on the concourse, the real estate agent whose firm was trying to sell Lincoln Inn and Lincoln Court came by with the latest in a line of prospective buyers. They had the place almost to themselves. As they passed us she bestowed a smile of sweet indulgence on me and Leo, as if our presence there lent quaint charm to the place. Eddie Braun, with a mug of coffee, crossed behind them from his shop and stood on the other side of the railing.

We watched them go into the empty space vacated by Craddock's. She made a sweeping gesture with her arm.

"What could she be telling the guy?" Leo said.

"'Unlimited potential,'" Eddie said, imitating her gesture with his free hand.

"'Crack security team,'" I said.

"And three unsolved murders still hanging over the place," Leo said. "Four if you count the old woman on the top floor of the hotel."

"The jury's still out on that one," Eddie said.

"Okay," Leo said, "three or four. Tell me how she finesses that."

"Easy," Eddie said. "This is America. Murder happens."

Omega floated down and landed nearby on the floor, regarded us with blank eyes, then pecked at some crumbs.

Eddie looked at the bird and shook his head. "There's a sales angle for you," he said. "Part mall, part zoo."

Mrs. Reverend Orville Sharpe marched by, her six kids, and finally the Reverend, strung out in her wake. One of her boys kicked at Omega, but it winged safely off and up.

"Think of it as a tradeoff," Leo said, "Brazelton for the pigeon. I say we came out ahead." He gave me a wink. "What do you say, Cleary?"

The Reverend, his combover out of place, looked over at us, his eyes, magnified by thick lenses, as blank as Omega's.

I shrugged.

"Amen?"

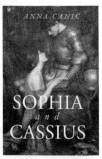
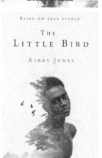